THE
BOOUKE

A Partial Fiction

In the unfolding of a person's life, the choice of a decision, to exhibit courage or the lack of courage by any man or woman when faced with a challenge, will not only affect their immediate family, but the lives of those to come in the next generations."

Dan W. Ingram

"Either define the moment, or the moment will define you."

Walt Whitman

Some Very Important Information
Please take the time to READ this.

In the course of human events, fate, maybe picks certain people to experience great moments in history, to receive large amounts of money, to be famous or meet people who entrust you with strange and fantastic knowledge. That's where I come in. Although my name is on the book, I am not so much the 'author' as much as I have become the "assembler" of this information. You are about to embark on a journey that will terrify you and leave you wondering about what is really going on in our present reality and what IS out there.

I was sitting at Starbucks one morning in my home state of Washington at a long table with several of us working on our computers. I couldn't help but notice the man next to me, to my left, was trembling and having trouble typing. He was sweating, wiping his brow and his breathing was very labored. This went on for about fifteen minutes when I felt the need to ask him if he needed some help or assistance. Little did I know that my one question would consume the next two years of my life and change my perception of reality forever.

This gentleman does not want to be identified for several reasons: He works for the government, he doesn't want to lose his job or be ridiculed and lastly, as close to a mental breakdown as he was, he doesn't want the pressure of the press, family or friends to harm his health. I respected his privacy and asked if I could share the story of his family and what he confided in me. He graciously agreed. We continued to meet at least once if not two to three times a week for coffee until we earned each other's trust. One day he invited me over to his house to talk more privately. I agreed.

The next week I arrived at seven a.m. at a gated community overlooking a beautiful valley with a postcard view of Mt. Rainier. I punched in the number at the box and as the gate opened I drove to his beautifully big natural rock house. I walked up and knocked as his house keeper opened the door and invited me in. She led me out to the veranda where he was sitting with his morning coffee and the *Seattle Times*. Standing up he met me, we shook hands and he invited me to sit down with a gorgeous view of the mountain. His house keeper brought me a Danish and a cup of coffee. After a while of chatting I broached the topic he touched on at Starbucks and was anxious to begin to interview him.

He said, "I don't know, Dan. Perhaps it is the luck of the draw of being in the right place at the right time, the accident of being born into the right family or simply chosen by a higher power to be the recipient of ancient truth and secrets. I believe my family has been chosen, to "bear this burden of truth," for almost one-hundred years and it's beyond me to know why."

He continued, "This secret knowledge, this information, in a hand-written journal has been passed down in my family for four generations from oldest son to oldest son. Only the oldest son, and none of the family members had any access to the journal or real knowledge of what I am about to share with you. Coming from my great-grandfather, William Jacob MacAoidh, this journal has only been read by four men, until now. Dan, do you think you are ready to have your perception of reality altered? You better think about it, because this is, well, big."

I sat there with the end of the pen in my mouth just staring at him, not saying a word, contemplating his warning. For some reason, I believed that his story needed to be told.

"Yes. I believe I would like to hear it."

"NO!" He said sternly. "I'm not talking about 'wanting to hear something cool!' Dan, I am talking about something that is so strange and big that it-will-mess-you-up! Are you ready for THAT kind of information?"

"Wow." I said. "Well, I have counseled a lot of people and issues in thirty-three years. So, I believe I can handle what you want to share with me and I believe I am open minded enough to receive what you are about to tell me. From our conversations in the past week I believe I can put your story out there if you want me to."

He leaned on the table and quieted his voice, "This truth that I've been entrusted with could be called a "strange and fantastic knowledge," by some, but that definition would be doing you and everyone else a disservice. The real truth and better phrase would be a "horrific, damnable and sorrowful" truth.

"Dan, the secret truth that I am about to reveal to you has been held within my soul and mine alone for over fifty years. Until I met you, I was about to go crazy and didn't know what to do with the information. I believe our meeting was meant to be. So, Dan, I am unveiling this for the first time to you, the first person outside of our family in four generations. I am going to show you this journal so you will know that what I say is not a simple tale of fiction.

"I also know that in revealing this that there are many who are experiencing similar events, that you are about to learn about, both as an individual and as a group. This truth is unknown to everyone except the ones suffering through it and occurrences like this are happening in the United States and all over the world. If you will, bear with me a moment and let me give you a case in point.

"Dan, have you heard of the Dyatlov Pass Incident?"

"Yes," I said, "but it's been a while, fill me in on it."

"Dan, listen, there were nine hikers who were ravaged at Dyatlov Pass in the Russian Ural Mountains between February 1 and 2, 1959. Their tent had been cut from the inside as if they were trying to see what was stalking them outside. Of the victims, one had skull fractures, two had major chest injuries and one had their tongue and eyes removed and two bodies found almost a mile to the north-east were frozen and they were only in their undergarments. They were trying to get away from something horrible. They even found a line in one of the female's journals that said, and I quote, "we now know the snowman exists."

"What?" I said.

"Yes, and, the last photograph in their camera, when developed by authorities, was so mysterious that most do not comment on it or at least dismiss it as a hoax or late addition. It's not. Trust me." *(As the author/assembler of this information, I have chosen to post the photo here.)*

Author's note: In my further investigation and examination I found that Dr. Boris Vozrozhdenny, who examined the corpses, concluded that three of the students died from fatal injuries so severe, that it was outside the realm of possibility that a human could have caused them.

The man charged with figuring out what happened was Lev Ivanov, a Soviet investigator. He had trouble coming to any real conclusions, so he decided to write that the students were killed by "an unknown elemental force which they were unable to overcome (Other translations state his conclusion as: "a compelling unknown force.")

A week later I shared this information with my source and he smiled and said, "An 'unknown compelling force' had caused the deaths. Yes, that is true and I know what that 'unknown compelling force' was and is."

Author's note: I have to say that this is NOT a story about "Big Foot," and you may or may not be disappointed in that. Although the truths you are about to learn may leave you wondering. As we continued to meet over the next many months I would ask him questions trying to 'catch' him in a lie or 'trip him up' because this is a big story. I never could.

I asked him one day, "How do you know these things you are telling me? Why reveal it now after almost one hundred years of keeping a journal of your families' information secret?"

He said, "All I can say is twofold: First, as I said earlier, my family was chosen for some unknown reason by a higher power to experience and be the stewards of this heavy and unsettling knowledge of secret truth. Second, as the current holder of this truth, somehow, I just know that this is the time and you are the person to share it."

He went on, "What is the purpose of my revealing this story, truth and knowledge? I have wondered that myself. Perhaps it is a warning? A harbinger of what is to come? Instructions for the future? I've come to think of this as the *information for the preservation of humanity*. Dan, what you and the readers do with this information is up to you. All I ask is that you not think me mad or a simple inventor of fiction, and that you make sure that your readers know I am a credible source and revealer of truth that I didn't ask to have."

As the author, I simply share the hand-written journal of my friend's descendant, telling of the unthinkable affair they encountered.

Again, as he said, it is up to you what you do with this information. Knowing what I know now, I would suggest however, that as you read it, keep one eye on the journal and the other outside on the weather. Oh, and if there is a knock at the door, well, I'd think twice before I answered it.

Dan W. Ingram
2019

"Words have no power to impress the mind without the exquisite horror of their reality." Poe

The true event from the hand-written journal of
William Jacob MacAoidh

Chapter 1

The Arrival

For whoever might find this in the future, these are the

last words and testament of William Jacob

MacAoidh concerning the community of Three Rivers

and its families. Being of sound mind and body I am

documenting our last day on earth. May God rest our

poor souls. Tuesday - October 29, 1929.

*As you are read*ing this, be so very glad you are

not here. I would not wish this on my worst enemy. I want

to encourage you right now to go hug your spouse if you

have one, your kids or your closest family or friends and

tell them you love them. For you never know when the last

day of your life is going to be, unlike me. I live deep in the

woods, two miles past Fetterman's Bog and I'm sitting in

my log house looking, for the last time, at the picture hanging on the wall of my wife and myself with our newborn daughter Madison. I remember the day we had that picture taken. But, first, let me fill you in on my family and the community of three rivers as I await certain death.

I was born William Jacob MacAoidh. Now, for those of you who don't know how to pronounce Scottish names Aoidh is pronounced A-o-id. My parents immigrated over from Scotland and I was born right here in Three Rivers in 1885 and I've lived here ever since. From a teenager I've loved my last name because I was told that Aoidh was a Celtic god of fire. In my youth I played and thought myself descended from a god and pretended like I saved my people from the dragon. "William the hero! William the Conqueror" I would shout! Oh, those were the care free days.

My parents Nevin and Elspeth MacAoidh lived in Glasgow all their lives. They were diligent workers and the economy in Scotland was good but there were so few jobs.

They talked it over and decided that there would be a better life and opportunity for them in America and for their children. So, they sold the very few extra items they had, saved up and bought two tickets and sailed from Scotland on the passenger ship S.S. Furnessia, from Glasgow and landed in New York, (Castle Garden) to be precise, as my mother wrote her notes, on Friday December 7, 1883. She wrote all these records down in her Bible for me to know after she was gone. The Master of the vessel was John Hedderwick, whom my mother wrote was a stern but fair man. I still have my mother's passenger list she kept.

ANCHOR LINE U.S. MAIL STEAMSHIPS.

Saloon Passenger List.

S.S. "FURNESSIA,"

John Hedderwick, Commander.

From Glasgow to New York.

VIA MOVILLE.

On FRIDAY, 7th DECEMBER, 1883.

Not long after their arrival and processing through Ellis Island, they were approached by a man named Robert who had a proposition for them. He would like them to come live in a self-sustaining community way out in the woods away from civilization. For some reason, the idea appealed to my father and mother and they took Robert up on the proposition. So, they moved here to Three Rivers to start their new life. From what I understand they loved it and never lived in regret. I'm glad they came, if they didn't, I never would have been able to tell you the wonderful part of my life that is coming next.

When I was 20, in 1905 I went to town with two other men of our community. We didn't go to town alone because we had to buy supplies and it took three men to load and make sure everything got back here safely and that no one was following.

It had been a cool fall day with a crispness in the air and the leaves starting to declare their majesty in glorious colors. Through the falling leaves, me and the fellers meandered over to get something to eat. Sitting in a small mountain town, the café was a charming looking store front with the words "Lorrie's Café" painted in red and white checkered letters diagonally across the big window presenting the tables and chairs inside. There was a beautiful glass case by the door that displayed homemade pies. Entering the establishment I was overtaken with the smell of coffee and baking bread. I walked up to the counter and ordered the Blue Plate Special for thirty-five cents and decided to pick up a newspaper on the counter for a penny to occupy my time.

I sat down at a table for four with my two buddies and it wasn't long before our food came. I should add here that, that was the best cooking I think I've ever had. I'll never forget what I ordered that night, it was the best bowl of pot-roast stew with biscuits and gravy.

Engrossed in the newspaper, *The Daily Herald,* I couldn't believe what I was reading. It reported that just the day before in Ohio, October 5, 1905 Orville and Wilber Wright flew a lighter than air machine for thirty-nine and a half minutes over twenty-four miles! I still wasn't sure I believed it. They say you can't believe everything you read in the paper these days. Besides. . . no one could go twenty-four miles in forty minutes. IN THE AIR! What is this country coming to? It was so magnificent to me, I kept the paper and have it to this day.

However, that wasn't the highlight of my trip to town. In Lorrie's Café that evening, I felt a feeling I have never felt before when the most beautiful young lady came over to me and asked what I was so excited about in the paper.

Looking up, I dropped the paper to my lap and was mesmerized. Staring into her blue eyes I simply said, "Huh?"

"What are you so excited about in that newspaper?" She was stunning. "Huh?"

"Why, I do believe you may be deaf as a stone. My name is Martha Innes." And she stuck her hand out to me.

I knocked my coffee over pushing my chair back trying to stand up to greet her properly. With coffee spilled all over my shirt and trousers, I grabbed her hand and said, "Please to meet you Ms. Martha Innes, my name is William MacAoidh."

"You're Scott?" She said.

"Yes, and I see you are as well, my lady." I slightly bowed my knee in honor and we both started laughing.

"So, what was in that paper that was exciting you so?"

"Do you know what Ms. Innes,"

"Oh, for dear sakes, please call me Martha."

"Very well, Martha, there is nothing in that boring newspaper that's worth talking about. Why don't we go over to that empty table and get to know one another. Would you be my guest?"

"I would love to, William."

I looked back at my partners with a smile and they just rolled their eyes and went about their business.

We sat down and both smiling, really didn't know where to start.

"So, Martha, tell me something about yourself."

"Well, William, before we do that, I noticed that you eat with your left hand!"

"Yes, I suppose I do. Does that interest you?"

With a slight smile and a glint of curiosity in her eyes she said, "I've only seen one other man in all my time here eat with his left hand. I thought it was very strange looking and here you are left handed. I simply noticed and thought it was cute."

Laughing I said, "Well to be honest, I've never thought of my eating with my left hand as being "cute."

"It is, but that's not all that's cute about you," she said with a smile and at the same time batting her eyes.

I tried not to swallow too hard as my mouth went dry and I could feel my heart beating like I'd just loaded a huge tree into the wagon all by myself. I'm sure I stuttered but I tried to change the conversation back to her.

"Well, I find you very attractive myself." She was wearing a light blue and white checkered dress that just showed her ankles. I did notice that. She wore a small black hat with one Pheasant feather cocked backward. That hat highlighted her beautiful red hair that almost left me speechless.

"Martha, could I buy you a piece of pie out of that case there?"

She began to laugh. "I don't want to be rude Will; can I call you Will?"

"Absolutely!"

"Well, Will, don't take this wrong, but I MAKE the pies! I have pie all the time."

"So, you are a baker?"

"I am a baker, a cook, a housekeeper...you name it. In fact, I am a very good cook!"

There were men sitting at the tables around us laughing at what I heard one of them call "young love" but I didn't care. I lost track of time and why I even came to town. All that mattered now was Martha Innes.

That was on a Friday. It was late and we had just arrived in town. We were going to retire for the night and shop all day for supplies on Saturday. I did not retire with the other two. Martha and I spent most of the night talking and getting to know one another. Eventually I made it in to my room late that night, or early the next morning, but not before Martha and I really hit it off.

I found out that her parents also came over on the same boat as my parents did. We don't know if they knew each other but we instantly had a connection. Her parents however, got sick on the eighth day of being on the ship during the fifteen-day trip to New York. They developed a red spotted rash and a very high fever. They were both quarantined at Ellis Island and stayed in the New York hospital for over three weeks. Martha remembers her mother telling her that the doctors said they were going to die because there was no cure for the unknown disease they had. As her parents were laying side by side in the hospital waiting for the other to die, all they could do day after day was to lay there and hold hands from bed to bed.

Martha's parents must have really caught the heart of the nurse, because at the end of three weeks, as they were about to die, the nurse asked her mother if there was anything she could do for her. Martha's mother took her up on it and asked her nurse if she could find her dear friend she made on the ship coming to America. The friend was an Irish woman who was a cook, named Mary Mallon.

After two days of looking and asking, the nurse did find Mary and brought her to the hospital to see Martha's mother. They sat and visited in the evenings when Mary got off work. This went on for several days and miraculously Martha's parents began to improve, lose the rash and the fever began to recede. After the fourth week, they recovered and were well enough to be released by the hospital. It wasn't until 1907 that we discovered that Martha's parents were the unfortunate friend of Mary Mallon. It was in that year that authorities discovered that Mary was the first healthy carrier of Typhoid Fever in America. The papers were full of articles about "Typhoid Mary" and how as a cook she was spreading Typhoid Fever and didn't even know it. Now we know what Martha's parents contracted on the ship and the miracle it was that they survived and Martha was born.

After their recovery, her parents found themselves an apartment and jobs. Two years later just like me, Martha was born in 1885. When she was ten in the winter of 1895, her parents got sick again, at the same time probably from the residual effects of the Typhoid. They both developed pneumonia and died within two weeks of one another. She was totally heartbroken and crushed. Martha was alone with just her father's sister to raise her, which wasn't saying much because her aunt like to hang around saloons and "stay out late" leaving Martha to fend for herself. It's a good thing she found favor with Mrs. Lorrie because she began to feed her and eventually took her in as her own. Martha started calling Mrs. Lorrie, "mom." From that time on, Martha literally lived in the café helping as a waitress and cleaner. That's how Martha noticed me as a newcomer in the café that night.

The next day we did all our shopping but my mind was on Martha. We bought, loaded and trekked back to Three Rivers. I left town riding on the clouds!

The community of Three Rivers would usually send three men to town only about four times a year but I promised Martha I'd be back next week. I didn't tell the men, I knew they would say no. When next Thursday rolled around and I told Pa where I was going and why. He didn't like the idea but smiled and understood and said he would tell Ma after I was gone. He would also tell any of the others who might ask where I was, that I had some business to 'tend to' and that was it. We all respected each other's privacy in Three Rivers and not much was questioned when Pa spoke. Everyone respected Pa's words.

Well, I came back to Three Rivers on a Monday but I wasn't alone! We had gotten hitched! I told her about our community and she agreed with everything and wanted to come and live as my wife and we've been happy as two pearls in a clam ever since!

Chapter 2

The Baby and the "Secret Society"

After setting up house in Three Rivers as husband and wife we had a wonderful life and Martha fit in fine with the ladies and they accepted her as if she had been born into the community. As time went on we lived our normal lives and Martha wanted a baby so badly, and really, I did too. We had trouble conceiving and after two miscarriages we were very heartbroken. Finally, in 1916 we had our first baby, a son we named James, a healthy baby he was! We were so proud and after what we had been through, we certainly didn't take life for granted.

A few years later, six to be precise, in 1922 Martha was with child again and we were cautiously happy but everything worked out for our next baby too. Now, back to the picture I'm looking at on the wall of Me, Martha and Madison who was just two days old in the picture. We knew it was time for Martha to have the baby so we left James with our community in Three Rivers. We arrived in town, found a hotel and checked in. With Martha being so close to delivery, she lay still on the bed and I went over and found Mrs. Lorrie in her café and told her what was going on. She immediately took off her bird apron, washed her hands and told her help that she needed to leave and for them to take care of the place until she gets back. I heard a lot of groans from the men knowing that someone else was going to be doing the cooking!

One of the old timers yelled, "Mrs. Lorrie, I'll pay ya myself if you don't go and stay here to do the cookin'!"

Lorrie retorted back, "I'll pay YOU myself to quit whining and never come back again!"

Boy did that get a laugh from all the men in the café! She could hold her own.

Mrs. Lorrie came with me to the hotel and I surprised Martha with my guest! Martha and Mrs. Lorrie, her "mom", began to cry with joy as they saw each other for the first time in a long while. Mom stayed with Martha all through the birthing process and I'm glad she did!

We were so blessed to have our daughter with us as her mother had a tremendous complication as Madison was turned backward during birth. But that doctor, bless his heart, kept a calm mind and did whatever he had to do to get her turned around and coming out normal. When the bill was presented to me, I was glad to be able to pay it and

I gave the doctor and extra twenty-five dollars for doing a great job in saving our daughter's life. That was a lot of extra money a few years ago back in 1922.

After a couple of days, Martha recuperated and Madison, named after her great-grand-mothers maiden name, was doing well. After the second day at the hotel we decided to celebrate so we walked down the boardwalk to the photo shop.

The medium built man greeted us kindly. With a large smile and his hands clasped together he said "Welcome to Harold's Photography. How can I be of assistance to you today?"

He was in his sixties, nicely dressed in a white shirt, black pants and a red cloth band tied around his upper left arm. His greying hair was quite disheveled from coming in and out from under the cloth on the camera. He showed us a variety of backgrounds and Martha picked the one she wanted. We got into position and Harold said, "Hooooold still." He got under the curtain on the camera but came back out. "Nope!" He said. "Lighting isn't right. Let me check it again." We sat there patiently for quite a bit while he adjusted the lighting.

"There." He said. He got back under the cloth. The big brown wood box camera made a series of clicks and the photo was taken.

As he was preparing the camera to take out the glass plates for developing, Martha and I were talking privately, soft enough we thought that the photographer could not hear us.

"I can't wait to get back home and show off my little girl and introduce her to her big brother." I said with a full heart.

"I know," Martha said, "Everyone is going to be so excited in Three Rivers."

The photographer could hear us just enough to pick up the term Three Rivers but obviously he misunderstood and he said, "I couldn't help but over hear you a little. I've heard tell of a community somewhere way out in the boondocks called Three Rivers."

"Really?" I said curiously. "What else have you heard about them?"

"Not much," he said. "Just that I heard they were a secret society. I try to keep to my own business but if you want to know anything they always go to Oscar's dry-goods store. He could probably tell you more."

When he turned to remove the plates Martha and I just looked at one another with big eyes and a contained smile. We stood there waiting for his instructions.

"You in town for a while?" He asked.

"We're leaving tomorrow," I said.

"Well, come back tomorrow afternoon before five and you'll have your nice little family photo to take with you."

"See you then." Martha said.

We opened the door and was about to exit when he said, "By the way, where are you nice folks from?"

"Oh, we can talk about that tomorrow when we pick up the photo." I said.

"Ok…" he responded in a confused manner. "Whatever pleases you nice folks. Good evening."

"Good evening."

As we exited I said to Martha, "Listen, we need to go to the dry-goods store to find out what the people know or think about Three Rivers."

She said with a frown, "But we don't need anything from there and we don't have much money."

"I know, but I do have a couple of dollars. I'll go in and we'll look around and I'll buy a couple little things as I ask questions and get some information."   She nodded.

Entering Oscar's Dry-Goods we were greeted again and I said we were just looking around. A very large man, whom it was apparent that he was used to getting his way, came out from the back through the curtains and looked over the counter and the store.

The attendant said, "Everything is as you requested Mr. Oscar."

"Very good," he said without even looking at her. "Go take your break."

"Thank you, Mr. Oscar."

I walked over in his vicinity and said very casually, "Good afternoon. We just had our photo taken at Harold's and he mentioned something about a community called Three Rivers. It was new to me so I inquired and he said you might know something about it since they come in and buy from your nice store here."

"Why are *you* wanting to know?" He said gruffly.

"I sir, am a studier of history and purveyor of local knowledge. I believe this information might be of interest to me."

Angrily he said, "I don't like Three Rivers, the people or what they do there. That's all you nice people need to know."

Smiling I looked him in the eye and said, "I think there is more you know than what you're telling me."

"Look," he said harshly. "I'm trying to be cordial. Don't push me about Three Rivers. No matter what I know, there's nothing you can do about it."

"Well then, Mr. Oscar," I picked up a copy of the closest magazine I could find and held it up. "I will be forced to write in my article in Harper's Monthly what terrible service we received at the dry-goods store and how rude the proprietor was. I don't think you want that kind of press do you Mr. Oscar?"

With a look of shock, his eyes widened and began to change his attitude. Chuckling he said, "No, no, no I didn't mean nothin' by it. What do you want to know?"

"Whatever you know or have heard."

Without batting an eye, he said with a scowl, "Strange people out there. A secret society they are. They only come to town about three or four times a year, and you can never get anything out of them."

"Really?" I said curiously. "What else have you heard about them?"

He continued, "I've heard that they are some weird religious goofs and they use their children as slaves. They eat horse meat and are no better than the wild uncivilized

Indians." He was confident in what he was saying nodding his head in "factual" confirmation.

Martha chimed in, "Why I've never heard of such a thing! How could anyone survive out there and what would a God-fearing woman do in such a place?"

Leaning forward on the counter on his left elbow he got really close and serious and said, "That's what I'm saying. A God-fearing woman wouldn't be seen out there in that savage community! I've even heard," he looked around to make sure no one else was in the store, "ma'am I'm sorry to say this in the presence of a lady but I've even heard that they 'eat' people who wonder into their camp and they are never seen again."

Martha gasped as if to be so in shock she couldn't believe it. It was all I could do to keep from laughing.

The proprietor continued, "If'n I was you guys, I'd forget everything you heard about that crazy community and stay as far away from it as possible. Just live your lives as decent human beings in a civil community where people don't eat each other." He slapped the counter, frowned and nodded his head at both of us.

"Thank you kindly for the information. I'll take this little photo frame."

"That'll be ten cents, thank you. By the way, you said you write for the Harper's Monthly, where do you nice folks call home?"

Martha and I looked at each other. I turned to look at Mr. Oscar and said with a very stern face, "We, live in Three Rivers and I would advise you and anyone else not to come looking for us 'cause you never know when you might get 'lost' in the woods or 'eaten by a panther' never to return. And you sir, would last that panther most the winter. We wouldn't want anything to happen to you nice folks here."

I've never seen a grown man turn as white as fast as Oscar did behind that counter. He began to shake and couldn't say a word.

I smiled very nicely and said, "Have a nice day." We exited and as soon as we got a store or two down the boardwalk, Martha looked at me and said, "I didn't know you wrote for the Harper's Monthly!"

Shrugging my shoulders, I said, "I thought it was a nice touch and sounded persuasive. Besides, I think he really would have lasted that panther most the winter!" We broke out laughing!

That night, the third night, we were going to stay at the Gold Digger hotel in town but Martha's "mom" insisted that we stay at her house and the meal that night at her café would be on her as her baby gift! What a treat that was. We thanked Mrs. Lorrie, for being with us during the delivery. I'll say again, I've never tasted such biscuits and gravy in my life! Martha was a little perturbed at me at how much I talked about Lorrie's cooking since she fancied herself a pretty good cook, and she is! I knew I was up against a wall, so I dropped it and shut up.

The next day she and Lorrie talked about the new baby and did some catching up on old times. Lorrie wanted to know all about Martha's new life in Three Rivers but according to our rules, we were very vague in our description and talking about it; even to her. The more Lorrie asked questions the more Martha began to stutter and look at me for help. We talked in generalities and Lorrie knew it. I changed the subject a few times and finally I said, "I swear Mrs. Lorrie, I do believe you were wearing the same birdie apron seventeen years ago when I first came in to eat." She agreed that she was and we had a good laugh. Eventually we had to leave, so after a sad good bye we left. On our way out of town we went back to Harold's Photography shop.

"Good afternoon! Welcome back to Harold's! Your photograph is ready and waiting!" He went to the back and brought out an envelope. He opened it, pulled out our photo and asked our approval. We loved it.

"That will be one dollar for the sitting fee and twenty-eight cents for the photo please."

I paid him and said, "That is a very nice photograph. Thank you."

"Well, thank you! You're welcome," he said. By the way, you said yesterday you'd tell me where you're from. May I inquire again?"

"Martha," I said. "Would you like to tell this nice gentleman where we're from?"

With a beautiful smile Martha didn't say a word. She looked down and reached into her bag and pulled the frame out we just bought at the dry-goods store. The photographer just stood there confused by her silence but he didn't say a word. She inserted the photo in the frame and asked the photographer, "How would you say this would look hanging on our wall in our home town of Three Rivers?"

His jaw dropped open and said, "Ma'am I'm sure it will look very lovely!"

We smiled and thanked him. The photo has been hanging on the wall in our home in Three Rivers ever since.

That's all I have now, remembering the good times we've had together and the trips we've taken. Now the reality hits me of how all of that is going to end today in death. With my gun in hand I keep peering out the window with frozen shattered breath. Not that it's cold outside, but rather, I am shaking to death with fear.

Chapter 3

The Confusion Begins

Just two days ago, on Sunday, we were all going about our normal Sunday routine. Pa, Joe and I were at Falls Flat, about two and a half miles south east of us where a good group of old standing timber was found last year by Dane when he was hunting for meat. We were scouting out the flat and decided it was certainly worth the logging with not too much effort of getting the logs out with it being pretty level. The pathway for the road would be easy to clear out without much effort.

All the other men, women and children of Three Rivers were relaxing, playing and visiting on Sunday morning as was the normal routine. Earlier that morning before Pa and I left for Falls Flat, Pa held a small Sunday meeting, a church of sorts. Most everyone came. Pa asked Dane to lead us in some Sunday hymns which consisted of several hand-written copies of the words of some songs from the one book we have; The 1860 copy of the

Philadelphia Presbyterian Sabbath School Hymn book someone brought with them years ago. We sang *Shall we gather at the river* and *When I survey the wondrous cross* while Robert's wife played the zither with our singing. After the songs, Pa brought a teaching on honesty from the scriptures. We were dismissed around 8:30 and everyone went about their own business.

In the middle of a quiet lazy Sunday morning suddenly, Doc, a shorter than average slightly rotund man who always wore red suspenders and black pants ran out into the square.

"Has anyone seen Elsa? Anyone know where Elsie is?"

Elsa is Doc Carl's wife and she was missing. Doc and Elsie (his pet name for her) got married and started a family later in life. Elsa is a tall slender very modest woman with brown eyes and higher cheek bones and a little darker skin like she might have some American Indian heritage. Her hair was long dark and straight that hung down past her shoulders. She was in herself a very beautiful woman. She has been teaching grades one through twelve for several years now and all the kids just love her. Patient, friendly and yet strict when she needs to be all the kids respect her, not only because she is respectable, but also because if they don't, they will get in trouble when they get home. For Mrs. Elsa to be missing is a big deal to everyone in our community.

Doc and Elsa have two boys, Matt who is eleven is a shorter stockier kid and Randy, sixteen is tall and slender with darker skin like his mother. They were running around yelling "MOM! Where are you? MOM!"

Robert sent Dane to get me, Pa and Joe. Dane rode up on his horse and told us what had happened. We quickly turned our mule team around and rode as fast as the terrain would let us back to Three Rivers. Pulling the team into the community, I secured the break and we all jumped off the wagon and ran to the gathering already assembled in the square.

Robert had called a meeting and organized our community into teams. He said, "Ok, the women folk will stay here in case Elsa comes back and the men will go out and look for her. We'll go by twos so we can be safe. Pete, you and Will head out toward Roller's Knob and circle back around the back side of the Landing. Adam, you and Joshua head out toward the Bog and come in by Big Tree. Dane you and Joe head toward Indian Hideout and come back by way of the Old Trail. Me and Shelby will make our way down to the Bear Den and head back by the Buffalo

Run. Doc we need you here in case anyone of us comes back with Elsa and she is hurt, you need to be here to take care of her instead of out looking for her. Fair enough?"

"Fair enough," said Doc looking around at all of us. We all nodded our heads at him with affirmation.

Before we left, my Pa Pete said, "Doc, can you tell us the last place you saw her and when?"

Clearly shaken with his mind running here and there in a fog of confusion Doc said, "I don't know…what time is it now?" Struggling at the smallest things, this time to get his pocket watch out of his vest.

"'Bout ten-fifteen," I replied.

Doc said, "Gosh, I can't even think. I don't know; boys do you know about what time it was?"

Randy said, "Dad you always go to your office at nine o'clock so it had to be around then."

As best as he could gather his thoughts Doc said, "That's right Randy, thank you. Elsa got up and fixed breakfast for us around eight. She fixed eggs and bacon with some fresh sourdough. I remember sitting there pouring Adam's sweet-bee honey over my biscuits. I don't know who can make better biscuits than my Elsie. She takes that flour and…"

"Dad!" Randy jumped in, "They need to find mom, can you just let them know the last time you saw her!"

"I'm sorry, um, we ate around eight I reckon and then we talked an hour over coffee about the boys and how school was going and I headed back to my office in the back of the house there like I do every morning and sat down at my desk promptly at 9 a.m.. I was in there doing some study and research for about, oh, I'd say maybe forty-five minutes. I got up and went to the kitchen to draw some water from the pump and noticed I didn't see her but that's not unusual. I thought she was outside hanging up clothes or maybe washing or even taking a short walk after cleaning up breakfast. I didn't think much of it.

I went over to the stove and got a piece of bacon that was left over from breakfast and just had a weird feeling. By this time, it was probably ten or fifteen minutes later and I went around the house looking for her, thinking she might be in the bedroom but she wasn't there. Then I went outside to all the places she could have been and she wasn't there either. Now I'm starting to panic! So, I began running around the house yelling for her and just couldn't find her and that's when I went into the square yelling for her asking if anyone has seen her."

He began to break down and cry uncontrollably, sobbing deeply. His boys were also crying rubbing their dad's shoulder trying to give some type of solace.

"Ok Doc, it's ok." Robert said, "We're going to look for her, you and the boys stay here and we'll be back when we find her or after dark. We'll do our best."

"Thank you, Robert. Thank you, men. You don't know what this means to me. I'm much obliged."

Robert said, "All of you, keep your taters up! Let's go."

We paired up and headed out. All of Three Rivers searched all day and late into the night. Everyone returned after dark exhausted and thirsty but no one had any good news. There was no sign of her. It was like she just walked off never to return or vanished but how can that be? No one can "just disappear!" We were all grieving and started to wonder 'what if'. . . (we felt that maybe this is the time for it), but no one said anything! "It," was the thing that nobody wanted to talk about. It was an exhausting day.

We all met out in the square by lantern light. With mosquitoes everywhere, the night was eased a bit by the cicadas singing and the few lightning bugs signaling each other that were left from the summer. We held a meeting and shared what we found or rather didn't find. Doc and the boys were crushed. The worst news they could have received, they got. No Elsa.

Doc struggled to talk, "Are you sure you didn't find anything? No sign of struggle? Clothes? Nothing?"

Adam replied, "Nothing Doc. We covered this whole area. We are so sorry." Doc began to wail a little louder. Pa, a rather skinny man who definitely does not "look" like a logger, but ever dressed in his blue overalls and white t-shirt and worn out boots went over and put his arms around Doc. He helped him up and walked with him over to Doc's house. Ma brought them some fresh bread and sweet milk.

After Doc returned to his home, Dane said to the other men gathered, "I didn't want to mention this with Doc here because it wasn't the time to say it but since Doc is gone and since it does have to do with the community, I did find a fresh new spring for our water not too far away and a lot of deer tracks for more meat this winter. Let's just keep that in mind."

"Good job Dane," Robert said.

Several other men chimed in and agreed that they found new deer sign too and they also thought about a good place to get meat for the winter. We broke up and went to bed ready to get up early the next morning.

I went to my house and took off my coveralls and bathed the sticky sweat off me. I put on my bed clothes and lay by my wife who looked so beautiful laying in bed with the dim candlelight reflecting softly off her ivory complexion and long red hair. Her eyes shot over at me and a slight smile came over her face.

She rolled over and put her arm around me.

"Will?"

"Huh?"

"Do you think she'll be found? Really?"

"No."

"That was a quick answer. How do you know?"

"I don't. But I just have a feeling. I'm afraid she's gone Martha. But worse than that, if she can be gone, I'm afraid. . ."

"What? Go ahead."

"I'm afraid, if she can be gone, then, *you* can be gone. And I can't imagine that. I just can't imagine."

She sat up on her elbow, got as close as she could to me and touched my nose with her finger and said, "I'm not leaving, William. I won't be gone."

"How do you know? You can't guarantee that."

"Will, my love is our guarantee."

Smiling I said, "honey, I'll take that. Thank you. I love you so much Martha."

"I love you too, William." We kissed more than a good night kiss and went to sleep.

Monday morning came early and the community started the morning by having breakfast together in the commons house discussing what happened yesterday. We planned to start the new day in a few minutes in our search for Elsa.

After a hearty breakfast of scrambled eggs, fresh sliced ham, grits of course, toast and good coffee, we broke up into our same teams again and headed out to the same spots Robert assigned us yesterday searching the whole surrounding area.

We looked, yelled, and made circles until about two in the afternoon. Nothing. Then, out of nowhere, we heard Joe Dilly yell.

"I can't find Judith! Judith! Juuuuuudith!"

Judith was Joe Dilly's seventeen-year-old daughter. She was a full-figured girl with blond hair. Not skinny but not overweight. Solid. Yes, that's the word, solid like her dad, Joe. A short stocky fellow but strong as an ox. I would never want to get into it with Joe or Dane.

As young teenagers, Judith and Randy have eyes for one another. They like each other but are embarrassed to be seen together. Judith is one of the smartest people I've ever met, even at her young age. I am very impressed by her, and now, *she* is missing! Two people are missing! Exhausted, we all hit the search trail again, same teams and same places.

As Pa and I began our search out towards Rollers Knob the third time, I began thinking and assessing the situation. I could see the whole community beginning to panic. There was constant chatter by the women while they were trying to console Carl and Pricilla, Judith's mother. The men, for the most part, we were all just quiet. Hurting deep down but staying strong and not saying much. Actually, we didn't know what to say. We knew "the time" was coming close but we never expected it now or to happen this way. For people to just disappear is unimaginably hard to understand. If they were killed or died, that's one thing but just to disappear, that leaves everything so unresolved, your mind is never at ease.

Like the other teams we crossed creeks, climbed hills, walked thru valleys looking in thickets, caves and so forth yelling for Elsa and Judith but again to find no one. I was so disheartened that all I could think about was my

Martha or my kids being the next ones to disappear. I must keep my thoughts on other things. I'll go crazy if I continually think about that.

We got to the end of our rounds and headed back to the community with bad news on our part but just as we arrived about an hour later Dane was coming up over the hill and we heard him shout, "Found her!"

Found her? Who is her? Elsa or Judith?

Topping the hill, we could see that Dane had Judith with his arm around her escorting her back gently. When he brought her back to the community, she looked like she was in a daze just wondering around not knowing where she was or what was happening. There was something different about her eyes. She had that 'far away' stare like she just wasn't with us in the present somehow.

All of Three Rivers were in a stir and gathered around her asking questions and wanting to see what was wrong with her.

Judith kept asking "What's going on? Why is everyone talking to me?" She couldn't understand why we were making such a big fuss over her. We told her that she went missing and Dane found her. We explained that Elsa was missing now too, not just gone, but missing and we don't know where she went. It just didn't seem to connect; until Judith nodded her head and said, "I saw her."

Running over to her Carl said, "What! What did you see?" Carl, unconsolably got in her face, grabbed her shoulders shaking her and kept asking through his crying, "What did you see, Judith? What did you see? Tell me girl! Did you see Elsa? Where did she go? What did...."

Judith was like a limp rag doll in Doc Carl's hands just sitting there staring and not reacting to the shaking and questions she was receiving.

Her dad Joe jumped in, "Doc! Doc! Get ahold of yourself! Calm down and let go of my daughter. Can't you see she's in a stupor? She can't answer you. She's dazed for some reason. Let go of my daughter right now!"

Doc turned to the rest of us and said hysterically, "Calm down? It's easy to tell others to 'calm down' when one of *your* family isn't missing!"

Tensions were running high. Joe Dilly, said, "Doc, this particular argument ain't about Elsa, it's about the way you are treating my daughter! You let go of her and leave her be!"

"She said she SAW Elsa get taken!"

"No, she didn't say she saw her get taken. She just said she saw her."

Doc continued, "I want to know what she saw so we can go get her. Make her talk Joe! She saw my Elsie taken!"

"Doc, I can't make her talk any more than I can make you calm down! What do you want me to do? We're all torn up about this!"

Doc said in anger with tears rolling down his face and snot coming out of his nose, "You're torn up? You got *your* daughter back and you're torn up?"

Joe was seething inside. His mind was racing on what he should and should not say. He knew that he could break Doc with one hand and probably should for what he was saying, but to Joe's credit he didn't.

Joe simply said, "Doc, you saw for yourself that I 'bout lost my daughter too. I ain't minimizing the loss of Elsa, but I ain't apologizin' for getting my daughter back. Although you deserve a good whoopin' we ain't gonna do that, 'cause you have a wife to find. Second, that ain't no way to handle things and besides all this, I consider us friends. You've made me pretty mad, Doc, but I reckon, if'n I was in your boots, I particularly think I might do the same thing. So, I want to say man to man 'I'm sorry.' Let's handle this like men and see what we can do to get Elsa back."

Joe held out his hand as an offering of peace and apology. Doc broke down sobbing uncontrollably and lifted his hand up receiving the gesture of friendship. Doc's breathing was erratic and he couldn't catch his breath.

I jumped in and said, "Doc, you know you need to slow down your breathing. We all care for you and Elsa and the boys and we don't want to see anything happen to you. Just slow down your breathing and catch your breath. Ok?"

Through his crying and sluffing he managed to get out, "Ok. I just don't know what I'm gonna do!"

Joe responded, "First of all Doc, don't you worry 'bout me none, we're ok. Now, let's just concentrate on getting these boys their mama back and getting you back your wife." Joe looked at the two boys and nodded in agreement that he was ok with them and they nodded back. They respected Joe.

Monday came to an end and we were all in a tizzy. Buzz was going around from group to group and everyone was very confused as to what happened and what we were going to do. We met at the council building sitting east of the square. Usually there is enough room to be comfortable with just the men and wives but this time *all* the kids were in there for two reasons; First, they wanted to know what was going on and second, the parents didn't want their kids alone out of their sight. I don't blame them because we had our kids in there as well. We agreed, we could not give up looking for Elsa so we decided to start early tomorrow morning. Everyone went to their homes Monday night. We could hear Doc and the boys crying all night long, even yelling for their mom periodically throughout the night.

Chapter 4
Tuesday – October 29, 1929

Today is Tuesday. We got up at six this morning to discuss the whole situation. Carl desperately wanted us to search for Elsa and we had decided to, when a slight stench started filling the air. That was not a good sign but it wasn't the smell of death. It also wasn't a smell any of us had encountered before. We were standing around discussing this when a green hue began to overtake the light blue dawn sky. Green? A green sky? Something was wrong and we all knew it. Instead of getting caught in a storm way out in the woods searching for Elsa, we agreed to wait it out a couple of hours till it passed by which grieved Doc even more. We tried to ease his mind by telling him that we could start searching again, by eight this morning.

This whole ordeal was so strange, that all the men would look at each other, in such a way; knowing the same thing, it was time; but no one said a word. Our hearts began to sink. It was silent, yet we were communicating with our eyes. Robert broke the silence.

"Men, the people of Three Rivers have faced many a hardship and struggle over the years. We are resilient…"

Joe Dilly raised his hand, "Remind me again what 're-cillient' means?"

Robert responded, "Resilient means we bounce back when we get knocked down. Now, we are not going to let this get us down or allow it to tear us or Three Rivers apart. I don't know if I've ever done this before, but I'm going to pull rank here. As the leader, I say that we all do whatever it takes to get along during this hour of crisis, or after it's over, whoever can't get along with the others, the council will meet, and decide if we need to ask you to leave our fellowship or not. NONE of this is our fault so we must stick together. Everyone got it?"

"Robert?" Joshua said.

"Yes Joshua."

Joshua continued, "I know I came here to stay and we shook on it. I get it. But that was years ago and Elsa is now missing and Judith just about went gone and honestly,

I don't mind admitting, I'm scared. And, although I've not spoken to any men in secret, I'm only speaking my mind for myself, I'm gonna guess that they are as scared as I am. I'm just a wonderin' if we shouldn't just pick up and leave and let this Boouke thing just have the place so we can have our families and our peace. I'm not suggestin' we leave straight up, I'm just thinkin' out loud. I'm willing to stay because of my word but I'm just throwin' it out there."

There were a few minutes of silence as men were listening and trying to process this whole ordeal. After a few minutes the silence was broken.

Adam responded, "Joshua, I respect your honesty and willingness to bring that up. That's a difficult thing to talk about in our community. It is true others have lost their lives to the Boouke in years past. Perhaps and probably most of us will today as well. However, I believe it's too late even if we all decided that was the best thing to do. And, like you said, we all shook on it. Like Robert said, this is none of our fault. Since Elsa is missing, I believe it would be a dishonor and mistake to leave with her gone. We're in this together. We put all our chips into the "game" if you will. We are invested here and although I do respect your thinking out loud, I say we stay here, do our best and stick it out. One way or another, we're gonna die here or there and here is where we made our home. I say we die defending our community instead of running."

There were some quiet barely audible agreements of "yeps" and grunts.

Joe Dilly chimed in, "I'm in favor of staying but I need to say something." His voice got a little quieter as he looked down at the ground. "As much as I hate to say it, I do believe that we're gonna die today if, this is the day." Now looking around at each of us personally, he continued, "I want to say it was a pleasure knowing each one of you and I couldn't have picked a greater group of friends to become my family. We all did what we felt like we wanted to do and it was good. We raised each other's kids, pitched in to help each other and along the line, each of us was nursed back to health by someone in our community.

"We've built a beautiful place to live and I'm proud to have known and been associated with each of you. I honestly don't know about the stuff Pete talks about, the afterlife, heaven and all that but from what Pete says, I sure hope it's true and I hope I have enough of that faith he talks about to get me there. Boys, I'm staying and I'll defend each one of you as my family to the death. You can count on me. If any of you survive and I perish, just know that it's ok. I don't have any regrets."

Joe cleared his throat and hesitated a moment and then continued, "I never heard my own Pa tell me what I'm about to say to you, and it's hard for a man to say this I reckon 'specially to other men. I don't know why, but it is. But I just want to say to you men here; I love you guys and I mean that from my heart. And, well, I guess that's all I have to say."

It was very quiet as all of us were trying to choke back the tears but not doing a very good job of it.

After a moment of composing himself, Robert said, "Joe, I think you spoke for all of us. Thank you." He went around the circle and addressed everyman for a yes or no as to whether they were committed to staying.

"Yes sir," every man said. For the first time, we not only shook hands but we all hugged one another. It was strange but felt good as we were truly a family. Unfortunately, it had to happen on the last day all of us had to live.

As we were standing around talking about this it seemed to ease the tension of the situation. Suddenly a green fog came falling straight down from the sky and started rolling in over the hill.

"Boys! Did you see that? A green fog just shot down like a shaft from those clouds! Just like a perfect column from the sky!" Adam said in shock.

"I've never seen anything like that!" Someone said.

"Holy frog warts!" said Joe.

Robert said, "A green fog?

Adam responded, "It looks like fog but somehow, I don't think that's fog."

Robert reacted, "This can't be a good sign for anything. Boys, I think it's time. For real this time."

"Doc," Robert said reluctantly, "I'm sorry, but we're going to have to postpone the search for Elsa because it's just too dangerous and we believe it's time."

"NO! You can't stop the search! We've got to find my Elsa!"

Robert said, "Doc, I'm making a decision. I can't risk the lives of Three Rivers right now with what's going on around us. Look at what's happening. We've looked for two days for Elsa and don't even have a clue. That doesn't mean we're giving up, it just means for right now, I'm ringing the bell and everyone is going to their homes to hunker down."

Doc said in anger, "I bet it'd be different if it was your wife who was missing!"

"I've made my decision. Doc, that's final."

Pointing his finger in Robert's face Doc said, "You know what you can do with your decision? You can go. . ."

"Dad!" Randy yelled. "They are not giving up. Let's just go home and we'll look again later."

Doc and Robert stood face to face staring at each other not giving any ground. Randy said, "Let's go dad, let's go home."

"It'd be different alright." Doc said as he walked away with his two boys.

"I'm sorry it had to come to that Robert." Joshua said.

"Me too. Hopefully he'll be ok." Robert responded. "Right now, we do what we know to do and, we know what to do."

We shook hands one last time and looked at each other knowing what this last good by meant. Each of us went to our homes, knowing what to do and this time, when Robert rang the bell, it *was* for *real*. Today was not a drill. We now know that this whole ordeal really started on Sunday, two days ago, and we didn't even realize it.

Chapter 5

The "Story"

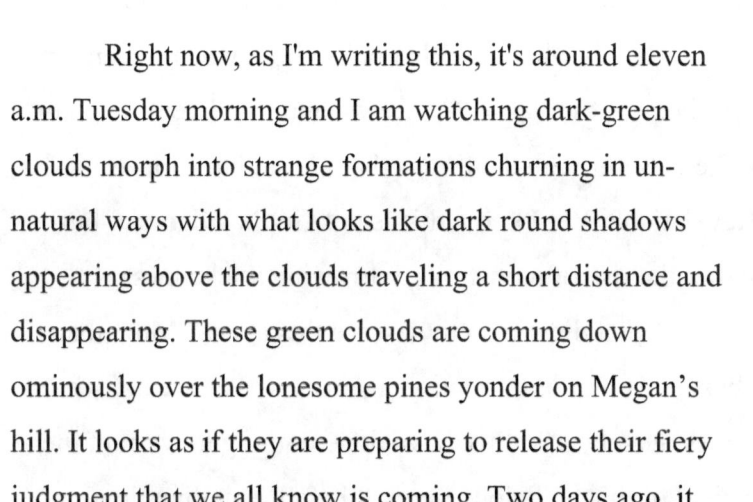

Right now, as I'm writing this, it's around eleven a.m. Tuesday morning and I am watching dark-green clouds morph into strange formations churning in unnatural ways with what looks like dark round shadows appearing above the clouds traveling a short distance and disappearing. These green clouds are coming down ominously over the lonesome pines yonder on Megan's hill. It looks as if they are preparing to release their fiery judgment that we all know is coming. Two days ago, it arrived, however, I have this sickening knowledge that today, the beast is about to make its big introduction to this generation. It is coming to bring certain death if it is at all within its power, and it is. Trust me, it is.

Years have gone by, dare I say decades if my memory calls, since the fates had last collaborated to unleash this dreadful pall. It looks like they've been talking and planning again, and the fruition of their scheme is about to happen. If there were just some way to be rid of these abominable fates so this terrible atrocity would happen no longer. However, the twilight of terror is awakening and I more than fear what we are about to undergo. The knowledge that today will be the last day for us on earth is not near as disconcerting as to *how* our demise is going to happen or where we will end up.

Is this what the Bible talks about when it mentions the "hour of tribulation?" Are we about to live through or rather, *die* through the things that are said to happen in The Revelation? Yet I know this is not God's judgment, but rather the rise of monstrous, harrowing wickedness.

What did we do to deserve this abuse? More than abuse, this murderous action against us? We are not white doves ourselves, but we have done nothing to warrant the arrival of this malicious fiend, this foul-smelling dragon. By the fates or the luck of the draw, we simply live here, on the spot, where it happens to come out. Of all places, we chose *the* place on earth to live where we are not alone. But we chose it out of good will and advice of the council. We had no idea what lay ahead, but we still chose it.

Hmm, the foreboding "musk" is thicker now, permeating the dense forest. Is this the smell of the beast or just a foretaste of its evil arrival? Or, is this the aftermath of its arrival two days ago when Elsa disappeared? Did our forefathers smell this years ago when this, what my Pa calls from the scripture, "The Abomination of Desolation" showed up then? There are no records, only oral traditions of the eradication. From what I see, sense and smell, this is the hour. That despised, dreaded, feared hour from which one only hopes and dreams to escape.

For most, in Three Rivers, if it goes as the stories of the horrible unspeakable past tell us it will go, this will be the last day with the gift of life we have on this earth. God help us. We will do our best to fight the good fight but how does one fight a force they've never seen and cannot see when it is here. How does one fight evil in its purest form? Strength? Pure determination? Perhaps it's both of those but there has to be a stronger power than evil to defeat it. That stronger power has to come from somewhere above. We need a 'higher' help.

It's been a good life I have to say, but I'm not ready to go. Just because the malevolent spirit shows up, I don't have to invite it to stay. On the contrary. I will be rude and do my best to make it leave, or even better; to kill it.

The story we've been told for years, about this evil goes like this; In the beginning God created the heavens and the earth. Lucifer saw how beautiful it was and wanted God's position. Well, God being stronger, He threw satan down to this earth and he landed right smack dab on the spot that Three Rivers was to be built 1000's of years later.

We live in the mountains past the hills and hollers and then another two miles, like I said, past Fetterman's Bog and evil has been dwelling here since Lucifer lost his first home. That presence, that no one understands, makes its power known in a very dreadful way about once in a generation, give or take a few years.

The story continues; Once Lucifer was cast from heaven he turned into the evil demon satan. He decided if he couldn't have heaven then he would have earth. So, he began to set up his evil minions to do his will. But once here on this earth satan faced an evil force within his ranks who wanted to claim this earth as its own and overthrow satan himself. Through a long battle, satan barely won. Because of its mutiny, this demented tormented evil was imprisoned underneath the confluence of the three rivers, under Hope Lake, in this long-lost out-of-the-way area. Satan has confined it to be bound forever under the lake, with one exception. Once every generation, it is allowed one week to roam free and exercise its free will.

This powerful source of evil has remained right here where Three Rivers sits, ever since. All we know is that this evil is called the Boouke. It's pronounced like "Luke" except with a "B". No one *really* knows who named it, what it is, where it comes from, how it gets here or when it's coming back. All we know is, that it's been happening ever since the dawn of creation and it's happening again right now and that that is what we are dealing with today.

Now you may wonder why people don't just move away from the mountain. But with all respect, I dare say that you cannot understand. One doesn't just "move" from where we live. First, it is too far back in the woods, we have our own community and to be honest, none of us would fit into a proper town and be comfortable as we've been here so long.

For us, it's our home. Why don't people move from places that have tornadoes all the time or earthquakes? This is where we live and we all live normal lives and like it. Listen, you just don't move if you live two miles past Fetterman's Bog. Even moving somewhere else on the mountain could not get you far enough from the Boouke, so our nine-family community just lives life right here.

But now, strange things are happening all around us. Every so often a window will grow dim as if a body were passing in front of it. Not blacked out like a solid body but just dim like a black fog or something. It keeps our heads turning and keeps us vigilant. It's hard to kill a shadow or a fog if that's what this thing is.

I will keep my mind occupied for now, writing about our experience. Somewhere, someone needs to know who we were and what we did and how we died. I don't want to be another 'Roanoke.'

Chapter 6

An interesting development

Oh! A knock on the door. No one is supposed to be out of the house! What is this? Suddenly a voice came whispering from outside my door.

"Will, it's Joe, can I come in, I need to tell you something." I went to the door to let him in.

"Joe! The Boouke Bell rang! What are you doing here? You know the rules! You are *not* supposed to be out of your house for anything what-so-ever! What's going on?"

"Will, I *have* to tell you something! This is important! Can I have a seat?"

"Sure! Let's set at the table."

We sat down at the table and I told him I am documenting all that is happening and why. He told me I could write down our conversation.

Joe said, "Will, after Doc and the others left my house, I sat Judith down, gave her some coffee and some pills to relax her. After an hour she seemed to be a little clearer minded. Me and Pricilla (his wife) began asking her questions in a very gentle quiet way."

Pricilla said, "Judith, you said 'you saw.' Did you see Elsa get taken? What did you mean? Can you tell me just a little about that so we might be able to get her back?" She sat there silent for a good two minutes, which is an eternity when you are needing answers.

"Will, you're not gonna believe what Judith said, and, what we found!"

I jumped in, "You *found* something?"

"Hold on Will, listen. Judith said, "I saw a shadow." It was so hard for me and Prissy (Joe's name for his wife) not to jump in and start asking questions but we remained silent for a good long time and just let her think, process and talk. She continued, and as she was talking, she never looked at any of us directly, but just a blank stare of sadness as she looked just over our heads at the wall behind us and continued talking.

"She said, "A shadow of a very large, tall big hairy man was leading me. I just followed him toward healing. Toward home. I had no choice but to follow.

"Then she went silent. Prissy asked, "Judith, what about Elsa? Did you see where Elsa went? Was Elsa with you?"

This time I was so engaged into the story, I jumped in again, "What did she say Joe?"

"Will, listen, you're not going to believe this; Judith said, and these are her exact words, 'No, Elsa wasn't with me, Elsa was taken from her house. As I was following the big shadow man, I saw her floating above her house. I continued following the hairy man by the path and over the hill. When we got over the hill, the big man just disappeared and that's when Dane showed up and brought me back here. Am I home?' Will, those were her exact words!"

I asked Joe, "She actually said she saw Elsa *floating above her house?"*

"Yes Will! Floating! What does that mean? I don't know? Will, she didn't even know she was home! Her mother said "YES, dear! You are home. Safe at home. Judith said, "I'm very sleepy now. Can I go to bed?"

Prissy said, "Yes, Judith, you need to go to bed and sleep."

"Joe," I said. "She kept mentioning a big hairy man or shadow. That's strange! Did she elaborate on that any?"

"No, and we didn't push her. She just talked about it like it was normal." He said.

"Look Joe, I don't want to be weird or anything but this sounds like the 'Ape Man' or 'Mountain Man' that the Indians talk about! I just didn't believe in any of that stuff and here is your daughter telling you he was there!"

"I know Will! I don't know what to think! I believe her and yet . . ."

I asked, "Joe, you said you found something. What did you find?"

"OH! I forgot to tell ya. Ok, so you know how clean and precise Elsa is about sweeping and so-forth?"

"Yes."

"So, I went to Doc's house. Him and the boys were inside crying and talking, they didn't even know I was outside. I looked around their house and in the commotion of looking for Elsa, there were so many foot prints around the front of the house, all the dust was just mixed up from everyone running in and out their door. However, I walked around back and coming off their back porch just off the last step down from their house closest to the ground, there was her foot prints. Two were by the step facing out like she was leaving the house."

"Ok, that's not unusual."

"I know, but, when I followed them off the porch and down the steps and out into the dust I noticed something. One, two, three footprints on the steps and then two side by side on the ground as if she was just standing there. And guess what?"

"What? Tell me!"

"Will, there was no more prints. She didn't turn around, she didn't retrace her steps, she didn't go on out into the woods, she didn't go back into the house. Just two-foot prints side by side in one spot and POOF! She was gone! But as strange as that is, you're not going to believe this next part."

"What?" I could hardly contain myself.

"Will, there were two of the biggest footprints I have ever seen right there with Elsa's. Huge! There were footprints pressing way down into the dirt that would make two of ours. If we put one of our feet in front of the other, it was bigger than that!"

"WHAT? So, what do you think Joe?"

"Will, if Judith was right, that MUST have been the 'Ape Man' and the spot where Elsa rose into the air and that's when Judith saw her floating above the house!"

"Joe. . ."

"I know Will! The other footprints."

"Joe, do you really think it was the Indian's 'Ape-Man'?"

"You know I don't believe in that stuff, but today, I saw the evidence with my own eyes. I'm here to tell ya, the size of those prints would scare the stickers off a porkypine!"

"Joe. . ." I said hesitantly.

"I know Will, it sounds impossible. But Judith was as calm and cool as a cucumber when she told us the story like it was no big deal. Will, she was not making it up. I just can't believe she was making it up."

I was writing as fast as I could and at times during his story, I would ask him to slow down or pause a minute until I caught up writing. I said, "Joe, I can't dispute you. Judith saw what she did and you saw what you did with the prints in the dust. I don't get it and neither do you, but we are dealing with something not from this world, I'm telling you."

"Will, listen, Judith said Elsa was taken *from* her house. I've told Doc so many times that he *has* to put taters around his house! This is the old wisdom, but *no*! He says. He's too scientific minded, he's too educated with too much schoolin' to believe in what he calls our 'religious voo-doo hodge podge'. Now look! The Boouke or Ape-Man or whatever it was came right up to their house, right into the heart of their family and brought Elsa outside without a trace! Dad-burn that Doc! We have to put taters around his house!"

"Joe, we have a covenant and agreement around here as you know. Certain things we all agree to and certain things we get our own choice. Doc just doesn't believe taters will keep evil away. Perhaps he will put some up now but we can't *make* him put them up on his own house! You remember the agreement we all made in council meeting with Doc. All of us agreed. Even you Joe.

"However, Doc still thinks Judith saw where Elsa went. I think we need to tell Doc exactly what Judith said so it might at least ease his mind so he won't think there is information hidden from him."

"Yes, Will, that's a great idea and besides it will help our relationship between me and him too. I believe we should go to Doc's house."

We got up from the table, *knowing* we shouldn't do this after the Boouke Bell had been rung but we agreed that this was important enough for Doc to hear.

I went and told Martha what Joe and I had to do. After some argument and hesitation, I told her I have to go and that I would be back. We were just going to talk to Carl, that's all. She agreed.

Cautiously and slowly I opened the door. We both looked around and took one step out on the porch. Nothing. We went outside with great trepidation and shotguns in hand.

Chapter 7

A Tough Decision

Before we left my house, I had asked Martha if she had anything I could take to Doc's family to help them out with food. She gave me some baked fish and a loaf of fluffy yeast bread. She begged me not to go, but I told her I must. This is for the boys and they need to know they are loved and taken care of.

Carefully and cautiously we walked over to Doc's house with shotguns ready. We could hear them crying and sobbing. I knocked and Randy came to the door and let us in.

Walking up to Carl I said, "Doc, Martha sent some fish and bread for you and the boys."

They said, "The bell rang! You aren't supposed to be here!"

"I know," I said, "but we have some information for you and your dad." They took the food to the kitchen.

"Thank you kindly." Said Carl. He got up and brought us two chairs to set on and we sat down.

"You know you aren't supposed to be here." He said. "Aren't you afraid of 'the Boouke" with all the scary tales you've been told!"

Ignoring his angry and sarcastic comments I said, "Doc, Joe here has something he needs to tell ya about Elsa."

"Elsie? You have news about my Elsie? Where is she? Did Judith tell you?"

Joe started in, "No Doc. Here is what Judith told us. When she finally settled down, we kept questioning her on what she knew about Elsa because we want to find her too. Doc, Judith won't say any more than what I'm about to tell you. Judith said she, herself, was led by a huge tall hairy shadow man over a hill. When we asked her if Elsa was with her or following the hairy man she said no.

"Doc listen, I'm going to tell you exactly what Judith said. It's going to be hard to believe and we don't understand it either but we think you at least need to know what Judith said."

Doc leaned on the edge of his seat and the boys gathered around to hear.

"Doc, Judith said Elsa was taken directly from her house and she saw Elsa floating above the house."

"*Impossible!*" Doc shouted! "That's the craziest thing I've ever heard! Floating above the house! She's delusional and lying!"

Joe stood up and said sternly with anger, "I'm trying to help you out. I didn't have to risk my own skin to come over here for you to call my daughter a liar!"

"Well you didn't loose your daughter like I lost my wife, did you?" Carl yelled.

"*Dad!*" Randy yelled through his tears. "They are just trying to help! Judith doesn't have to be lying! She's probably telling the truth!"

Carl answered back, "Judith said she saw your mother *floating* above our house! That can't physically happen!"

Randy continued, "Maybe it did! And *maybe* if you would have put up the taters like everyone else insisted, instead of trusting in your science maybe mom would still be here!"

"You listen here Randy!" Doc said, "This is not my fault, and I'm not going to take blame for your mother missing because I didn't participate in their voo-doo! You hold your tongue boy!"

As Matt was watching the interchange between his dad and brother, Randy said, "I'm tired of your science!

You're not even trying to work with the community! Dad, you can do what you want, me and Matt are going to stay with Joe or Will! You aren't even *trying* to protect us! I don't believe in your science! I want to stay alive!"

"You boys aren't going anywhere! I'm your *dad*!"

Randy and Matt ran out of the house immediately over to Joe's house.

Doc jumped up from his chair and ran to the door yelling, "Come back here! Boys! Come back here now!"

My Pa had heard the shouting earlier and, against the rules after the Boouke Bell rang, he walked over to see if he could do anything to ease the tensions. He was just standing around listening and cautiously looking with gun in hand.

Joe said, "Doc, I'm not one to get into family business, but I don't want you to think me or anyone else put them up to this. This was their own thinking. I don't know where they went but I don't want you to think bad of us where ever they went. It 'twernt' our idea for them to leave."

"Get out of here!" Doc said in a calmed quiet anger. "I've lost Elsie, now I've lost my boys. Just get out."

Pa took it on his own to come in and he stepped up and said, "Doc?"

"I said get out. That means you too Pete with all your religious voo-doo. Lot of good your God did for our community!"

"Doc just hear me out."

"Listen Pete, none of your 'Good Book' crap. I don't want to hear it right now."

Pete said softly, "Listen, this is about your family. Let your boys calm down. You're still their dad and they will come back to you. They are just upset now like you are. This is their way of dealing with it. Let them stay with Joe, they will be safe and you do what you must do. Then when this whole thing blows over, you've given them time to let off steam and they'll be back."

"I guess you're right. Can't bring 'em back anyway."

Pa gently said, "Ok. Doc, you gonna be ok? Want to come stay with me and Millie? You're welcome."

"No, thanks. I'll stay here and defend my house. I still believe in the sciences."

"Ok, well, Keep yer tat…. sorry, didn't mean anything by that, I'm just used to saying it."

Doc smiled a half smile, "It's ok. I know you didn't."

With Doc settled Joe and I nervously walked back to my house, sat down at the table and I continued recording our continued conversation.

Joe said, "Will, we have to get with Dane and find that hill and see what's over it. I know Judith said Elsa was taken from her home but we have to see where Judith was going and if Elsa is somewhere in a cave or something over that hill too. We must find the location of that hill. But I don't want everyone in Three Rivers going, we make way too much noise and besides the bell is already rung. It needs to be me, you and Dane for a short mission."

With a green sky and fog continuing to roll in, I sat there a moment in contemplation. Sighing deeply, I nodded my head yes and said, "Yep, Joe. For Judith and Elsa's sake, I agree. Let's go to Dane's house and talk to him."

Just as I started to put my pen down we were startled when another huge shadow crossed the kitchen window. It didn't cross it in one movement though. It came across and stopped in the middle of the window, move a little and then continued across. Whatever it was, it was big!

I said "Joe, you sure we should go out? It's against the rules of what we practiced and there is *something* out there! We've already been out once. Should we press our luck or go ahead and tell Robert?"

"Dang!" said Joe, "I don't want everyone involved, but, I reckon we need to tell Robert so someone will know what we are doing."

"Agreed," I said. "Let's go."

I explained to my wife what we were going to do and again she begged me not to go out.

"Honey," I said with all my heart, "We are all in this together. If you were the one who was gone, I'd expect others to go with me to try to find you. I must go. Listen, I will be back, you have my word on that."

Crying but with a stern backbone she looked me directly in the eyes and said, "How can you guarantee that?"

I responded, "Someone once told me that their love was their guarantee. My love and determination is my guarantee."

She started laughing and crying at the same time and said to me, "You better keep that promise William Jacob!" We hugged and kissed good bye.

Joe and I carefully opened the door and made our way to Dane's house. We explained everything to him and he assured us he could take us right to the hill where he found Judith. Next, we went to Robert's house. That was going to be a tougher sell.

I knocked on Robert's door. I heard him yell, "Who in the sam hill is knocking on my door after the bell rang! *Who is it?*"

"Robert, it's me, Will with Joe and Dane. We need in to talk to ya."

Robert scolded us, "*Don't* you know the Bell rang! What are you doing at my house? This ain't no Sunday stroll in the square. We've practiced this for years and now you decided to do whatever you want? This better be important!"

We assured him that if his wife was missing, we would do the same thing. Yes, we made our plans on what to do and not to do after the bell rang, and we practiced them, but we can't plan for everything that might happen. Elsa being gone, wasn't in our plans, but we have to do this, and still follow our plans we have set out. No one else in our community will know. Especially, Carl, as we do not want to get his or the boys hopes up. We will do this quietly."

Through parsed lips Robert said, "Boys, this is against my better judgment. I hate to say it this way, but I'd rather lose one instead of you three more. But, yes if it was my Virginia, I suppose I'd want you to do the same thing. However, here's my word, I want you to be back within the hour. Is that possible?"

Dane assured him it was since it was not that far away and he knows exactly where to go.

"Ok, go with my blessings. But! Be back within the hour! Got it?"

"Yes sir." We all agreed.

"Boys!" Robert said.

We looked at him to hear his last statement.

"Keep your tater's up."

"You too." We all responded back.

Chapter 8

The Hill

I brought my notebook with me trying to write as I walk. This green fog is really something. It has an odor to it but I don't know what it smells like and it's thick. It's not like regular fog where you hand goes right through it, this you can actually seem to move as you push it with your hands.

I don't mind saying this is scary, leaving my family at home while shadows appear outside my windows and I am not there to protect them. I said a silent prayer under my breath, "God please protect them during his hour."

Before we left, I asked the two of them if I could lead in a short prayer. They agreed and Dane surprised me when he suggested that we join hands as we pray. I started, "Father, we ask you today to protect us, help us find answers and Elsa too if she is still around. Help us to get back to our families safe and please protect our families as we are gone. Amen."

"Amen" they said.

As we set off with Dane leading, we could hardly see anything and the fog and with the thickness of it, it also made it difficult to breathe, especially with the stench that was coming from somewhere. Dane was one of our hunters so if there were anyone who I wanted leading us it would be him.

He started out with confidence and we were silent as we eased our way through the green lit woods and fog. Turning left at this rock and trekking up and down hills not knowing which hill was the one. Our senses were so heightened that the slightest noise almost took our breath away. We knew, that we were sitting ducks out here in its territory.

Dane asked us if we noticed that there were no birds flying around, no animal noises, no breeze just total silence. Only wood's sounds like branches popping. It was strange to hear no frogs croaking, no crickets chirping, no bug noises of any sort, just dead silence. It was like the forest had been emptied of all life but us three.

After about twenty minutes, Dane said, "I've been this way no telling how many times, but I'm outta' sorts with my directions. I know where I think I am but we should have come to the hill by now and according to my calculations, we ain't."

He was genuinely perplexed. I know I can get us back home but I thought I could bring us right to the hill I found Judith on.

"Do you think it's the fog messing you up?"

"No, I don't think so. It's just that the hill doesn't seem to be here. As soon as I found her, I looked around and got my bearings and noticed landmarks and none of those are here."

"Or at least as far as you can see." Said Joe.

We walked a little further and heard a stick snap in the distance. It was a big stick and a short distance away. We all immediately froze. We held our breath, barely allowing air to come in and out so that we could hear and so nothing would hear our nervous breathing. Someone, or rather something was walking through the woods not far ahead of us.

Dane listened intently. He said in the quietest voice he could, almost not talking, "That's not a deer, not a racoon or opossum. I don't know what that is and I live out here in the woods!"

We sat down there in silence a good five minutes and we heard it walking in a circle all the way around us, circling us as if sizing us up for lunch or trying to determine which one of us he could get first. I have never been so scared in my life.

We each had our back to the others all looking in different directions in case it decided to attack. We were all shaking and scared.

"Let's go left just a little more," Dane said.

We stood up and moved left, up a slight incline. When we got to the top we heard a whispered, "Ah Ha! I think we're here."

"Look! There are signs of footsteps or where feet shuffling in the leaves are going down the hill. That might be Elsa's trail!"

We all three squatted down again on our haunches with our backs touching in a triangle looking in all directions and thinking. The fog was so thick we couldn't see where the steps went.

"Let's mosey real quiet like down the hill just a few yards as see what we see." Dane suggested.

Joe whispered, "I don't think that's a good idea. We're already being tracked and circled, I think we need to mosey on back home."

Dane said, "Will, you're the deciding factor. What do you say?"

"Well, I say I guess we come this far, we're in it up to our necks so let's do what you suggest and head down just a few yards only then make our way home."

"Ok, I'm in." Said Joe.

We made our way down with an eye on the time. We'd been gone about thirty minutes now and we needed to be getting back. Constantly looking, we didn't see anything out of the ordinary. *Movement*! Just a few yards in front of us! We froze. Our breath sounded as loud as locomotive chugging across the tracks. We tried to breathe softer but it was difficult with the adrenalin flowing through us. Our guns at the ready, we stood there like statues. What we saw wasn't recognizable, just a quick glimpse of a huge dim shadow through the green air, but there was movement in the trees like we spooked it.

Oh! It stinks all of a sudden! "Did you hear that?" Joe said quietly?

"Yes" said Dane. "I heard it."

When they saw the movement, I was too busy writing so I didn't see it but something caught my ear. "What was it?" I said.

Dane responded, "A short growl then a huff.'"

"Yep. Exactly what it was." Said Joe. "Came from directly in front of us. In fact, I see a dark opening up yonder. Is that a cave or just a dark rock?"

We eased a little closer, the hair on my neck was standing on end. Something was here. Sure enough, it was a cave. Dane said, "Well I'll be. I've never seen this cave before. How could I have missed it all these years? It's like it just opened up!"

We approached the opening and peeked in. It seemed as if the cave had a soul all its own. You could feel a living presence from within. *Stench*! "Elsa?" "Elllllsa." Nothing. Oh! I heard it *that* time! A louder growl with a huge huff at the end.

I said, "Listen, we're thirty-five minutes out. We know where this is, but we promised Robert we'd be home in an hour. We have to head back. There is no sign of Elsa right now but we can return."

They agreed and we eased back making as little noise as possible. We kept hearing movement behind us and short bursts of growls but we kept watching and moving. Every so often we heard a 'knock' like sound of two sticks hitting one another or a stick hitting a tree. It was hard to tell.

We turned and began our trek home. Just a few yards from the cave opening, suddenly something burst forth right in front of us! It was coming toward us, so fast and, in the fog, we didn't have time to see it. Joe and I went left and Dane went right and a huge giant dark creature leapt right through the middle missing all three of us. We started running and high-tailed it out of there. As we were running we looked around to make sure we all were still there and Dane was gone! Joe and I put on the breaks! We heard Dane yelling, "Help me! It's dragging me away! Come back! Help me!"

We turned around and ran back and there was Dane on his stomach, flat on the ground being pulled backward toward the cave! We caught up with him and there was nothing pulling him but his legs were up in the air. He was just moving backward as if an invisible force had ahold of him!

Joe and I grabbed his hands and both of us felt a shock of electricity go through our bodies, but we didn't let go. With all our effort we dug in our heels and pulled with all our might. All of a sudden Joe was knocked away from Dane and fell about ten feet from where he was. Only I had a grasp on Dane's hand now and the force, whatever it was, was pulling both of us to some unknown destination as we were screaming back and forth to each other with encouragements and instructions. We had been pulled about thirty feet when Joe got up and back to us and grabbed Dane's other hand. Again, we dug in with both our heels and pulled with all our might and I yelled, "God give us strength!"

All of a sudden, we felt another bolt of electricity run through us and then we felt Dane break loose of whatever had control over him. The force of the release of his body propelled all of us backward and we were all on the ground. With leaves and twigs going everywhere, we scrambled to get up. Once up, we started running through bushes and creeks, limbs and stickers. In our running and panic we saw a huge shadow run ahead of us faster than we could even think of running. It stopped and was standing in the direction we were running as if to stop us.

Dane yelled, "Right then left!" We all started running right and as the creature did, we immediately ran left and got around it. It screamed and we heard a tree being pushed over behind us as if it were angry. Still running with all we had, we heard it growling and grunting behind us. Rock and limbs were being thrown at us and one rock hit me in the back of the neck and I tripped but kept my balance and stayed running. Joe had had enough, still running he simply pointed his pistol behind him and fired a 'warning shot' at it. We think it might have been hit as it yelled a different yell right after his shot and we didn't hear it behind us anymore. We didn't quit running for almost twenty-five minutes before we made our way back to the community.

We fell to the ground in the square wheezing and coughing and gasping for air for what seemed an eternity before any of us could even breathe normally, much less talk. None of us could get enough air. Our sides were hurting so bad because we could not breathe. It was like we were drowning out of water! Our heads were pounding from a lack of oxygen and our legs felt like rubber. We could barely stand when we did get up several minutes later.

Robert heard us and was already looking for our return. He ran out and said, "What happened? I heard a gunshot!" Still we could not talk.

After a few minutes, Joe said, "What *was* that?"

"I don't know!" I said. I didn't see it but it 'twernt nothing I'd want to meet again!"

"That, boys, was a monster." Dane said. "We got too close to its home and he didn't like it. We were almost monster meat."

Joe responded, "You mean *you* were almost monster meat! What was pulling 'ya Dane?"

"I don't know! I was running with you guys and all of a sudden, I was on my belly being dragged backward and it was so fast that I didn't know what was happening and it took me a minute to yell. I'm glad I did! Boys, I literally owe you my life. I can never repay you. You risked your life for mine!"

I said, "Brother, that's what we do around here. We take care of each other. We're just glad you're ok." We were all three still on the ground talking. We didn't have the strength to stand up yet.

"Get up y'all." Robert said, "It's too dangerous out here. Come into my home and tell me what you saw, then git back to your own families and hunker down."

Struggling to get up, and barely able to walk, we quietly went into Robert's house and had a cool glass of water. After catching our breath, we explained what we went through and Robert just shook his head back and forth in disbelief.

"Yep, we're in for a long ride gentleman. Don't know what we can do but hunker down and protect our families as best as we can. Keep your tater's up!"

We said the same and made our way home after hugging one another. We were safe. Momentarily.

Chapter 9

The Community

Problems in the American government, economics and unemployment were the reason the community of Three Rivers was established nearly one hundred years ago by Robert's second great-grandfather Omer Scottsdale Lee. He had a dream way back in 1833 to establish a self-sustaining community consisting of eight to fifteen families that existed away from society and operated independently from the government. Mr. Lee's handwritten charter for starting Three Rivers with the original families and signers is hanging on the wall in the Commons House. We look at it like our Three Rivers Declaration of Independence. In our community, in sixth grade every child is taught American History AND the reason why Three Rivers was established and how we maintain a community. Since you didn't go through school here I'll give you a brief insight.

Every child in sixth grade must pass a memorization test of the Three Rivers Charter. I will cite just the beginning for you:

Let it be known, that we as citizens of this great United States of America, in the year of our Lord 1833, desiring to live under the authority of the Constitution, have found conditions in our country intolerable for the preservation of our families due to poor economic decisions by President Jackson.

Let it be known, that we are not insurrectionists, and do not support rebellion or revolt against our country.

Let it be known, that we recognize our Constitution as authority and it grants us certain unalienable Rights, that among these are Life, Liberty and the pursuit of Happiness.

Because of these rights and because President Jackson refused to renew the charter of the Second Bank of the United States, causing the banking system to collapse, resulting in a national panic, banks to close and jobs to disappear:

And as an assembly of families agreeing to covenant together to take advantage of our right to the pursuit of happiness;

We Resolve: In order to form a more perfect union for us, to establish Three Rivers community, away from society and exist as a free and independent self-governing people free of our government banking system within that community.

We Resolve to live under the Constitution and U.S. government law anytime we are outside of our community.

For almost one hundred years this charter has served Three Rivers well.

The families that come in and go out of our community is a unique event. Over the years, people of course have died by natural causes or sickness which thins the population. Other times, according to our Three Rivers Family Roster and History Journal, within the last one hundred years, five families over the years have decided they could not take it. They packed up and left. Whether they made it, we don't know. We put time, energy, effort, into establishing them as part of our community and when things got a little hard or difficult or years were lean; instead of pitching in and everyone coming together, they decided they were going to leave.

We highly value and need our privacy. So, when people have decided to just leave, there is a private meeting with them in the Commons House with three men from our assembly and the family that is leaving and the children if they have any. Let me say there are certain private things that we have sworn to secrecy within our group. What is said in those meetings is one of those secrets that we hold close. I honor that and will simply say, I cannot share what is told to those families who leave Three Rivers but I can say every family who has left under those terms has agreed to the conditions that were put before them when they left. So far, we are still a free and independent self-governing people after all these years.

The citizens of our community have done a very good job over the last century of keeping things quiet about our association.

Most people die out of our community, five have left. . .then, there's the Boouke. Every generation or so, give or take a few years, we get thinned out quite a bit by the Boouke. Then we must go to town and recruit some more families to come live in Three Rivers. It's not the easiest thing to recruit people to come to a place where they will very likely meet their death. Sometimes we have more families, sometime less but we manage well with about nine to eleven families. Otherwise, if you come to Three Rivers, you are expected to die at Three Rivers, it's that close a family.

We got our name because as you might guess, there are three rivers that come together and meet right outside of our community. No one knows the real name to these rivers anymore but the founding fathers of our community named them Faith River, Perseverance River and Free River to remind us that faith and perseverance will keep us free. The Perseverance runs right by our community and meets the other two about a quarter mile from us to form a great confluence we call Hope Lake. Good fishing.

The Indians have a saying that at the point where three rivers come together you can count on two things; First, no tornado will ever hit there. Second, that's where evil lives. I'm here to tell you as I live and breathe today, those two things are absolutely true.

Most every conversation in Three Rivers ends with the phrase "Keep your tater's up!" Whenever any young un' asks what that phrase means, the answer is always "I hope you'll never have to know" and that is the end of the conversation followed by, "keep your tater's up." This didn't seem strange growing up here, especially when everyone in your world is raised that way.

In our community there are nine occupied houses. The homes are arranged fairly close to one another, about thirty feet apart so that if anything were to happen it makes for a kind of fort where we can shoot between the houses and still remain rather close. It also allows for downright cozy living and we all have to get along. There is a million acres or more I reckon around us, so if any of us gets stir crazy we can go in any direction as far as we want.

The homes are log cabins with mud and cement between the logs. They were built many years ago and every so often we all pull together to do some repairs, replace a log, chink a hole or repair a roof. They are great to stay cool in the summer and they keep us warm in the winter.

All of us have been in each other's homes for this or that and they all kind of resemble each other with family pictures hanging on the wall or decorations. Every home has the shotgun hanging right above the door. Some homes have a picture of George Washington or Abraham Lincoln hanging above the mantle. Others have pictures of loved ones past who served in the Civil War or World War I.

Every house has a porch that runs the front of the house and some go around the side which makes a nice shaded place to sleep or eat. Flowers adorn most porches with them sitting on the railing or hanging from the ceiling.

We have a well that was dug many years ago and each house contains a pitcher pump at the sink to pump our own water from the well which is very nice. We used to have only two outhouses, men and women but a few years ago we got together and now each house has an outhouse behind the home. What a nice convenience, our personal bathrooms! Everyone was so excited and boy did we have the jokes to go around when we were digging and building each outhouse!

Right now, everyone and I do mean everyone, (except for one hold out) has strings hanging all around the edge of their roof line. On the end of each string is tied a nail and a fresh potato is pushed on to the nail. Ten potatoes hang from each side of the house. Inside the house, down from each bedroom door hangs three potatoes and three hang down from every window. We are vigilant, when the potatoes start to die and shrivel and turn brown, we take those off the nail and use them as planting potatoes. We put a new fresh potato on the nail so we always have nice green taters hanging up.

With nine families we have three loggers, me, my Pa and Joe Dilly. You would not figure Pete, my Pa, for a logger as skinny as he is but boy can he hold his own and he knows everything you ever wanted to know about logging. He and ma have me as their only son. I'm not that big either but I can hold my own with the logging skids, chains and the mules. Martha and I have two children who are the delight of our lives! I've described them to you earlier.   Joe Dilly is, well, Joe Dilly and he is one of the toughest men I've ever met. He and Pricilla have two girls, Judith and Anna. Judith is sixteen and Anna is fourteen. Both of these girls are beautiful young ladies.

I've already told you about Doc Carl and his family and their dilemma. What a terrible shame. Doc seems to be the weakest and most timid of the men living in Three Rivers. I would have to say at medicine he is very smart but as a person he is very intimidated. I believe he has low self-esteem and struggles at his 'manliness." As kids we used to love to sneak in his office window and put a small garter snake in his desk drawer and every time he pulled it open, it would scare the wits out of him. We always got in trouble for it but it was worth it to see the Dr. scream like a girl then get mad.

Three men do all the hunting and fishing for meat, they are: Dane, Shelby and Robert. Dane is the tallest biggest man I think I've ever met. He stands about six foot five and weighs about 210. He has thick dark wavy black hair and is a muscle of a man! If I fought either Joe or Dane I'd quickly get pummeled but if it came down to it, I'd rather fight Joe than Dane. Dane always wore a red checkered shirt that he said was good for hunting because the animals could not see red. He was a great hunter. No one over the years has killed more meat for the community than Dane.

The last two men work our four gardens, Adam and Joshua. Adam is the most soft-spoken man we have in Three Rivers. He is a medium built guy with a small belly on him with sandy brown hair on the sides and back and is balding in the front and on the top. He is the animal tender to the chickens, goats, hogs, plowing horses, logging mules, three milk cows and a hutch of rabbits. Everyone else also pitches in and helps take care of all the animals.

Joshua is the youngest of the men in our group. At twenty-four he is a hard-working mule. He's not afraid to do anything and for anybody. His long red hair waved in the wind and every once in a while, I hear the women ask how a man can get such beautiful hair and all the ladies get left behind. Everyone likes Joshua.

Robert Lee is the leader although decisions for Three Rivers are made by the Council of Men and wives.

Robert is totally bald and a tough codger. He also wears blue overalls and always has a piece of candy for the kids throughout the day.

Then there is my Ma and Pa and they only had me. I always noticed they looked older than the parents of the kids I used to play with my same age but I never thought to say anything. Didn't matter I guess. They were my Ma and Pa and they love me.

My Pa is the most religious one of the group. He is always referring' to the scriptures and the Bible and how Jesus helps him get through things. I'm not sure the other men have completely bought into it, but they do notice a difference. Every time one of them has a problem or something they need to talk about and figure out, or as we call it in our community, "going to cipher something out" they always come to my Pa. He has a lot of wisdom and a gentle spirit the Bible talks about.

All the men respect each other but I think my Pa holds a special place in Three Rivers. Whenever there is a hard question or a final decision, eyes always turn to my Pa and someone usually asks, "Pete. Whatcha' thankin?" Then my Pa will take the straw out of his mouth he'd been chewin' on for the last hour and he'd give his thoughts.

He is a careful man, always weighing out his words and carefully formulating what everyone said then he usually has at least two scripture verses that somehow go exactly with the situation we are facing. None of the men can figure out how he always knows what to say and how he knows so much scripture that he has at least two for everything. Sometimes just joking one of the men will call him "Parson" or say, "Thanks Reverend." My Pa just smiles and says, "That's what it says in the Good Book and that's good enough for me."

I was certainly raised with the Bible teaching and I wholeheartedly appreciate it. It wasn't shoved down my gullet, but we read the Bible and we prayed at meals. Pa was *always* asked to say the grace at community meals. He'd never fail to get a little "preaching" in through one of his good *long* prayers. The people said it always seemed like they'd been to church after Pa prayed. Some said because it made them feel so good, others said because it took so long to finish. Pa just smiles and says, "That's what it says in the Good Book" and now, everyone chimes in together and says, "and that's good enough for me." We all have a good laugh. Everyone in our community knows that sayin' by heart.

Pa also would make sure to tell everyone, and we heard it in our home a lot, "The Word of God will help you through tough times. That's why it's important to know the scriptures." If I heard that once I've heard it 10,000 times, "The Word of God will help you through tough times." My Pa has a lot of sayings.

We have a good community at Three Rivers. We know each other's strengths, short comings, buttons not to push and all the generosity. There is hardly ever a disagreement or argument. If there is, it is more between the husbands and wives than anything. Then one of the men might come to my Pa and they'll 'go out to do some cipherin'. Everything's all right when they get back.

Maybe once a month, maybe every two months Pa holds a little Bible study for whoever wants to come. It's certainly not required like our council meetings are. Most everyone comes to Bible study, unless there is sickness, it gives us something to do and talk about. We have great discussions about life questions and what the Bible has to say about it. We don't argue doctrine because no one really knows what they believe. We just ask questions, Pa goes to the scripture and answers them and then someone will think of a question and we'll go from there. They are great studies that usually last two to three hours.

The wives are so dear to us. They work as hard as we do and more with the cookin', washin', havin' kids, takin' care of kids, dishes, and putting up with us men folk. They are strong helpmates to each of us. We men talk big when we're by ourselves, but we mind our p's and q's when we're around our women folk. They are the backbone of our fellowship in Three Rivers. All I can say is, I'm glad I'm a man. I don't think I could be strong enough to be a woman.

We have three extra houses right now that no one occupies. We use one for storage, one for a Commons House and one just stays open for whatever is needed. There is also a building for the school house. Even though our homes are close together, there was a bell hung years ago that rings three times every day to start school, come in from recess and to end school.

The schoolhouse is one room that goes from first grade up to twelve or whatever grade the oldest student is in at the time. The room has a big potbelly stove in the middle to keep the kids warm in winter. We have a chalk board that has the pictures of Washington and Lincoln above it and each child has a slate tablet to write on with their slate pencils for penmanship, homework and such.

Mrs. Elsa has been our Schoolmarm for many years. She wants to be strict but has a heart that just loves the kids too much, (if that's possible). The kids love her but I will have to say that she does keep good discipline in the classroom. All the parents have told Mrs. Elsa, that if any of the children act up in a way as to need a paddling, all she has to do is leave the school, walk over to the home of the child acting up, get the father and *he* will do the paddling. So far, she has never had to leave the class and walk to any home, although she threatened me once, when I was in school, I am embarrassed to say.

Writing all this and remembering the good memories is helping me to keep a calm head and keeping my mind off of whatever evil has come this way.

My heart is racing again just thinking about it. My hand is trembling, and my breath is getting shaky. "Dear God, if You can find it in Your heart to help our community through what is about to come, we would be very much obliged. Thank You kindly."

We've kept a community countdown over the years, but quietly. We knew the Boouke would come but we didn't want to let the kids grow up knowing and thinking about the fact that they would face death sometime in the future. We knew, but we didn't think about it. We just lived life and enjoyed company. Every day of our lives, the potatoes reminded us that this day would come.

The first few years after the Boouke arrives, does its damage and leaves is called the 'count-up'. There is a lot of grieving by those left behind. Houses have to be cleaned and ready for the next families who are going to be recruited. If there are any bodies left there are the burials to do in the small grave yard just to the east of our community. If Three Rivers is to continue, those left have to go out to town and talk to and recruit families to come live here. Then there is always the work left to do because some have been taken by the Boouke and that work still has to be done. Animals have to be fed, meat has to be hunted, gardens tended to, logs cut etc. The first couple of years after the Boouke leaves is very difficult. The second several years are called the 'count-down', life is ok. But approaching year twenty-five is very stressful. We know it's coming. It has no rhyme or reason, just sometime in a generation, give or take a few years.

We don't even know the approximate year. Stories have been told that it can be thirty-nine years before the Boouke comes up to forty-two years. Other stories have said twenty or fifty, we just don't know. But believe me, we adults live in fear and trepidation. Looking over our shoulders, watching out for each other, it gets tense and emotions are on edge. Emotions run high when you don't know when something dreadful, that will kill you is coming, but you know it is.

If we had to talk about it, we had very strict rules. No adult ever like talking about the Boouke.

Chapter 10

Shhhhhhhhhhhhh!

Growing up, the Boouke was not mentioned in public. If it was mentioned at all it was only behind closed doors while the sun was up and NEVER at night. Ever. Oh, and on the days of a full moon, not even in the day time. Never.

My Pa and Ma showed me so much love and compassion. I could not have asked for better parents. I could talk to them about anything. They were up front and honest God-fearing people. They were always eager to hear what I had to say or what I had learned out in the woods. We talked for hours, open and honest. That's my Ma and Pa.

My Ma is a shorter heavyset lady with bigger hips than the other ladies in our community. She almost always wears an apron and her face has the wrinkles from years of smiles and friendliness. It's easy for Ma to smile. I hate to say it but her fingers are beginning to be very painful for her and they are starting to grow sideways and the knuckles are getting very large. It really pains her and she rubs them constantly. But it will never keep her from cooking or hugging those she loves, and she loves everyone! She is a strong woman.

As for me, the thing that marks my life I think is that as a child, for years, I kept having re-occurring dreams and memories of some tragic event I must have blocked out of my mind. It involves another house and me being in a dark hole and hearing screams. At least once a week if not twice, I would dream someone was holding me and they were running through a dark tunnel with lights all around it. I was being bounced around and suddenly I was thrown into a dark hole and the top lid would slam down and scare me. There I was, in a dark hole, not knowing why or who put me there or how long I would be there.

In my dream I could see up through the cracks between the lid and every time I look up, a green light passes over the lid then goes away. It's always a green light. Then suddenly, I would be in another house beside my own that I live in. It was the same house every time but I don't know where or who's house it was. I could see people but their faces were not recognizable. I could hear talking but I could not make out what they were saying. I would wake up breathing so hard, with sweat on my head and sitting straight up in bed. When I was younger, it scared me so bad that I wet the bed a few times when that scary dream came. The dream always embarrassed me, that's how bad it was. Over and over year after year I would have the same dream.

I remember thinking as a small child, what if some night, I dream this dream and the green light, which I knew somehow was bad, would stop and get me. What would I do? That scared me to death when I was little.

One summer, as a teenager, for weeks I had been thinking about talking to my Pa and Ma about it but it seemed dumb to me to be so disturbed about a simple dream. Yet, it bothered me so much that I decided I was going to ask them. So, I got up the nerve and brought it up one night at dinner conversation. I don't know what this has to do with it except I remember exactly what we had to eat; fried deer steak with mashed potatoes, gravy, fried corn and cabbage and fresh bread and sweet milk to drink. As good as the meal was, I picked through it and they saw that something was bothering me.

"What's wrong Will?" My Ma asked gently with that gracious smile of hers.

I began to explain my dream in complete detail without leaving anything out and how I felt. As I was talking about all this, something strange happened. Right after I mentioned it, things got real quiet and a somber look

106

of hesitation arose in both their faces. Pa quickly glanced at Ma who immediately stared down at her plate without looking up.

Pa lovingly put his hand on my shoulder and said, "If it's ok, we'd like to discuss this tomorrow when the sun comes up. Is that ok Will?"

"Yes sir." I said. I wondered silently, what could it be that we could not discuss it tonight? Tomorrow? When the sun is up? What do they know that I don't about my dream?

Pa smiled; Ma got up to wash the dishes. I saw Pa wipe the newly formed sweat off the rim of his brow. He then walked over to the end table and gently put his hand on the Bible and said a silent prayer with his eyes closed. He walked on over to the outside door and stopped. Looking up, he checked his shotgun hanging above to make sure it was loaded. All that night I could hardly sleep, thinking about what they knew that I didn't. Why was it so bad?

The next day precisely at high noon, Pa sat with me at the table while Ma presented freshly made molasses gingersnap cookies with a glass of cold sweet milk. There was my Ma, easing everything with a bit of flavor. As she sat the milk in front of me, she smiled a smile that I knew was very difficult for her. It wasn't her 'normal' smile and that told me something was coming. I sat there in silence listening to Pa and he began to tell me the following story.

Pa said, "Son, we knew this day would come and it came way too fast." They looked at each other and smiled. A very serious look came over Pa's face.

"Will, when you were just a wee lad, something happened here at Three Rivers that we call a 'Massacre of eradication'. It comes around about every generation, give or take a few years and it was time for it again when you were about 5. It poured out it's damnable fury on our community. Inside your parent's house…"

I jumped in, "My parent's house? What do you mean, my *parent's* house?"

"I understand your questions Will, just let me finish. The Boouke made its appearance in our community. It was going crazy and inside your parent's house it was chasing you and your mother. She threw you into the potato cellar under the floor at the last minute. We believe your human scent was masked by that of the potatoes and . . . Dear? Could you make sure the door is shut and locked?"

"Yes, it is locked now." Said Ma.

"Thank you my dear. As I was saying, your human scent was masked by the potatoes and the 'Boouke,'" he said with a quieter voice, "could not smell you and passed you by."

"The Boouke? I thought those were just scary stories the boys told to scare each other. You mean the Boouke is real?" I was stunned.

Pa got the most serious face I've ever seen. He leaned forward toward me and said in the quietest most serious voice I've ever heard him talk in, "Son, I don't want to scare you but what I am about to say is the truth and you need to hear it and know what we are up against.

"The Boouke is as *real* as you and me. It is more than evil. It is diabolical, vengeful, murderous beyond measure. It kills to kill. It lives to kill, it breathes to kill, it's whole being and purpose is to kill and eat people flesh and drink people blood and take people to places no one knows. Yes son, the Boouke is very *very* real. Never doubt the reality or power of the Boouke. As soon as you do, you're dead."

My Pa continued, "After the ordeal was over, those of us who were left got to talking. We found out that all the survivors were either hiding in the potato cellar or the potato crib. We just figured that since that's the one thing that the survivors had in common, that the potatoes either hid the smell of our human scent to the Boouke or it didn't like potatoes. So, we decided on that day that everyone who lived in Three rivers from now on would hang the potatoes around every home and in every room for safety."

"Pa, Doc don't have no taters around his house. I thought you said everybody had to?"

"Well, son, that was a point of high tensioned discussion. When we recruited the Doc to come to Three Rivers, we already explained everything to him about the Boouke and what happened and what we reckoned about the potatoes. However, the more he got to thinking' about it, the more ridiculous it sounded to him. Here, let me get the minutes of our council meeting and read them to you." Going over the book shelf, he grabbed a brown covered book with red binding. On the outside of the spine it said LEDGER. They used a ledger book to keep the minutes. Opening to a certain page Pa said,

"Here it is. Ok, let me find it. Yes. Ready?"

I shook my head yes.

Pa continued, "Robert Lee said: "Pertaining to the fact that everyone who survived the last extermination of the Boouke, I recommend that every house in Three Rivers hang potatoes to a standard to be determined so as to keep out or mask our sent from the Boouke, whenever it arrives again."

Joe Dilly, "I second that."

Robert: "All in favor say "aye""

Families: "aye"

Robert: "Any opposed with "no.""

Doc: "No! No! and No!"

Robert: "Doc, seems you are pretty opposed to this little hope that we have to keep the Boouke away. Care to explain to us the reason for such a 'no' vote?"

Doc: "I'm an educated man of the sciences. Making me put up "raw spuds" around my house to keep away 'evil' is the silliest thing I've heard of. There is no scientific empirical hypothesis to prove evil or that potatoes would keep it away even if it did exist. If you want me to believe this, bring me pragmatical evidence that supports your hypothesis that is considered empirical, tangible evidence."

Pete: ("That's me, I was taking notes.") I said, "How do you spell 'hypothesis, empirical and tangible? And what do they mean so as I can record them here in this minute's book for others who read later?"

Doc: "For Pete's sake…"

Pete: "Yes, I was the one who asked." (I laughed.)

Doc: "No, that's just a saying. Hypothesis means an educated guess. Empirical and tangible mean something real if you can taste it, touch it, see it, hear it or smell it. If you can't give me that kind of evidence on how the spuds or 'taters' as you call them can keep this evil (that you can't prove) away, then I'm not playing this childish game of 'voo-doo-hodge-podge' with the spuds."

Pete: "Doc, I don't know about empirical and tangible, but I do know that the Boouke came and kilt a bunch of us and those of us who were in the potato cellar or bins were the only ones to survive. Is that empirical enough?"

Doc: "Coincidence! This 'Boouke' as you call it, just didn't see you in the cellar. That's why it missed you. Making me put up spuds against my will is equal to making me believe in a religion you might force upon me. I didn't come here for that and I'm not going to do it."

Robert: "Men, let's convene together without Doc and discuss this option for Three Rivers."

Robert and us men came back in an hour after talking together with this report: "It has been decided by all the men that we shall honor Doc's request not to put up taters around his house based on personal opinion. We believe this will not endanger the rest of us but if he chooses to endanger his own life or family then that is his decision as a man in Three Rivers. Therefore, although it is highly recommended, it is not a mandate by our community for anyone to conform to the potato hanging for protection. Our only request is, Doc, that if the Boouke comes again, and you don't have the taters up, may God have mercy on your soul. We don't condemn you or look down on you. You have made your decision and we will live with that and the men have been instructed not to mention it again. Is that fair enough Doc?"

Doc: "Men I'm proud of you for making that decision. I didn't think you would vote that way. I appreciate it and respect your ideas of feeling like you need to put up the potatoes. As far as God having mercy on my soul if the Boouke comes back, well, I put my faith in the sciences and will trust in what I can see. Thank you, men. As far as I'm concerned, if you are through with the topic I am as well. We will go on from here and be friends and good neighbors."

Robert: "Good enough for me." And all the men agreed as well.

Pa said, "So, son, that's why Doc doesn't have taters around his house." Pa closed the Book of Minutes and put it back on the shelf. He continued with my story.

"Will, I am very sorry to tell you this son, but the Boouke got all your family and you were the only one to survive, like I said, because your mom threw you into the potato cellar under your floor. After the ordeal was over we ran around Three Rivers hollering and trying to see who was left and we heard your voice in your potato cellar. There was not a trace of your family. They were just gone. There were no clothes left or torn, no sign of struggle, no blood, nothing! That's what happens a lot of the time when the Boouke shows up. You were crying hysterically and latched on to Ma like she was your real mother.

She looked at me with that look of raised eyebrows and I knew what that meant, especially since we didn't have children of our own. I smiled and nodded my head yes. Your mother started to cry and laugh at the same time. I've never seen her so happy and proud and sad at the same time over what just happened as the day you came to live with us. We decided to raise you as our own child. We knew you from the time you were born here at Three Rivers and watched you grow up to that point and thought a lot of you and your own Pa and Ma. We were good friends. It was just natural that we should do that for them and for you.

"You asked a few questions when you first come to live with us but eventually, they became less and less, and it was just like we were your Ma and Pa and we all accepted it and you seemed to fit in real well. I want you to know that your Ma and me love you very much and are really proud of you."

I don't think up to that point, I had ever seen my Pa right up cry, but he was crying real tears. There were tears in everyone's eyes. I just couldn't hardly take in what I was hearing and I was having trouble talking through the tears and lump in my throat.

"Pa?"

"Yes." His gaze now fixed on the table and he was 'twiddling his fork as if to brace himself for what I might say.

"How. . . did they. . .?"

"We don't know son." Again, he and Ma gave each other a glance. "When it showed up, everyone just hid and then we heard a long drawn out low growl. Someone screamed and then they were just gone. When it happened, we could identify one or two by their voices. Then, they were just gone with no blood, no torn clothes and no bodies. It's as if they never existed at all, just gone. They don't ever come back."

"Are they eaten up, or taken somewhere?"

"We don't know. They are just gone." His voice got quieter. "Just. . . gone. When the Boouke came back in

1890 no one saw it. We saw shadows go across the window that scared the be-jeebers out of us. It was a huge shadow looked like a huge man taller than tall, like eight or nine foot tall. I glanced out the window to Ma's protesting and I saw this big dark shadow of a man like creature, large and hairy but I could not make anything out. I know this sounds like a fairy tale but I'm telling you, it's not son. This thing is real. We would hear growls and screams and then people would be gone. That's all I know to tell you."

My Pa was the strongest Man I knew. He was strong because he was a logger. But he was also a strong man in his faith and strong in his determined will. But in this short conversation I began to see a hint of fear in my Pa's eyes and face I'd never seen before. Not weakness, but frustration that he was so helpless and at the mercy of the Boouke. At the very best he could do, he could not even assure the safety of his family against this pure evil.

"Son, I told you I'd do my best to answer your questions. Do you have any more for me now?"

"What were my mom and dad's name?"

Pa said, "Your own Pa was named Connor and your Ma's name was Meaghan. They were immigrants from Scotland. What a fine 'luvely' accent they had. We loved listening to them tell stories of Scotland."

"What was my last name?"

Pa answered, "You were William Jacob MacAoidh. Your father used to tell people very proudly that Aoidh was a Celtic god of fire."

"So, I'm Scottish?"

Ma said happily, "You sure are Will!"

"I'm descended from a fire god?"

"Well, I wouldn't go that far," Pa said, "but if you want to play and pretend that you do, that's ok with me! Oh, I just remembered, it's been a long time. Dear, would you please get 'Will's Memories.'"

"My memories? What does that mean?"

"Thank you dear. Will," my Pa continued, "Here are the things we gathered from your parent's house that we thought would be of importance to you when you came to manhood, as you have today. Here is your father's pocket knife. It's called a 'Bartender's Lock-back'. It's a good one."

I looked at it as if it were the Holy Grail itself. It might as well have been. But then he presented me with more of my memories.

"Will, here is your father's hunting knife. It's different than ours here in America. This came from Scotland and it's called a Dirk. Isn't it nice!"

"Oh, my." That's all I could say. I had never seen anything like it. "It's Beautiful. This was my fathers?"

"Yes Will, those were your fathers. And, here is your mother's Bible with all her notes and dates and letters to you when you were little. These will be very valuable to you. They thought a lot of you Will. You were their pride and joy!"

Ma spoke up, "I remember the day you were born, Will. We were all so excited! Your mother was so beautiful even in the middle of having you as her first baby, her countenance, was so calm and she was just a beautiful woman."

"Who do I look like more? My mother or my father?"

Ma and Pa looked at each other and they smiled both agreeing that I favored my mother in my looks but my father in my strength. I felt so proud at that moment.

Pa handed me a folded piece of paper and said, "Will, I want you to read this privately, in your room. It's just to you. When you go to bed tonight, I want you to read this with all the love that the one who wrote it had for you."

"Ok. I will." I took the note gently and didn't quite know what to do with it.

"Pa, you have always told us to put our faith in God. How come we hang the 'taters' trustin' in that to protect us instead of God?"

"Son, that's probably the best question I've ever been asked and it's something' I've struggled with too. However, let me put it this way. When we take a trip down to Hope Lake and we're having' a good time talking' and walking' but we're going through bear country what do we do?"

"We talk loud and make noise as to scare away the bears and not sneak up on them and surprise them so they won't attack us."

"Right. Now just because we do that, does that mean we don't also trust God?"

"No…"

"That's right. The bears are naturally afraid of human beuns' and God gave us a natural defense against the bears, that is us being loud as so to scare 'em off. So, if the Boouke has a natural affinity against 'taters, and we know that, shouldn't we also use what knowledge God gave us against this evil?"

"That makes sense, Pa. I reckon."

"Sure, it does. My faith in God is still as strong as ever, but that don't mean He can't use a 'tater or two to help us if the Good Lord decides that's what He wants to do."

"Pa, I just don't know how you have answers to all the things that come up. You are the smartest guy I know."

"HA! HA! HA! Listen Will, smarts and wisdom are two different things. I ain't the smartest person, but I do pray for wisdom. Wisdom is the ability to use the smarts that God gave ya in a good way. I like to say God has made me a little wiser in my older years."

"I hate to ask this Pa, but what IS it?"

"We just don't know son. It's just pure evil but we have no defense against it. We don't know. Any more questions?"

"No sir. But I reckon that this is a good time for me to say thank you for all you did for me, and my own Ma and Pa when you really didn't have to. I appreciate it very much. I love you."

Ma chimed in, "Yes Will, we had to. When you were left an orphan, it was meant to be that you would be ours and we wanted to. You weren't a burden, you were and are a real blessing."

Pa got serious again, "Ok, here is what you need to know now." He looked at me like man to man and continued, "Son, you need to know that today with this conversation and information, you've become a man. I'll let the rest of the men know and now you are allowed to talk to any of them about this, but just know it's up to them if they want to talk to you about what we talked about today. You have heard the rules, and yes, the stories and the rules are true and real. Only behind closed doors, when the sun is up and never...,"

"I know Pa, never at night."

He sat and just stared at me. He smiled and said, "You're a man." Then the smile disappeared from his face and a concerned look came over him. "Yes, son, today you have become a man." He got up and went outside. I heard Ma crying in her bedroom. Pa came and stuck his head back in the door. "Son?

"Yes Pa?"

"Keep your taters up."

"You too Pa."

There is a sayin' around Three Rivers that goes like this:

"Everyone will face
the Boouke once in life.
But blessed you are
if you face it twice.
Blessed to face twice?

This evil renown?

Yes, blessed you weren't taken,

the first time around.

In my case it didn't get me the first time around. However, as I'm writing all this down, I don't feel so blessed right now.

Oh, about the letter. I've always kept it in my secret possession and it was from my mother.

Dear William,

I have waited nine months to see your beautiful face. You have stoated around inside my stomach for the last six weeks before you were born. I had a mother's feeling you were going to be a boy, and I was right. I could tell you were going to be strong like your father! I would rub my belly feeling your head wondering who you were going to look like. After you were born, you only cried a wee bit. I held you up to my breast and you smiled and slept next to my skin with your long eye lashes. So small you were, but as we say in Scotland, 'Guid things come in sma bulk.' You were a guid thing! Your father was standing staring at you, scared to hold you but with tears coming down his cheeks. He was so proud of ya. Proud that we had a son! You're only a few days old now but when you read this letter always know that no matter what happens, along with your

father, our love and our spirit will always be with you.
When you are lonely I'll be there with you. When you need
courage, your father will be there with you. William, you
are a MacAoidh! The son of Connor MacAoidh. Go
conquer dragons and kill beasts! My little warrior William,
you can't read this now but someday this will be
meaningful to you. Our Gaelic blessing upon you our son,

> *May the road rise up to meet you.*
> *May the wind be always at your back.*
> *May the sun shine warm upon your face;*
> *The rains fall soft upon your fields and*
> *May God hold you in the palm of His hand.*

We love you William Jacob MacAoidh! Remember, we are
always with you. Our love. Your Father and mother,
Connor and Meaghan MacAoidh.
June 29, 1885

I still cry every time I read that letter. "Dad, I need your
courage today. I need you. I wish you were here with me."

Chapter 11
Waiting

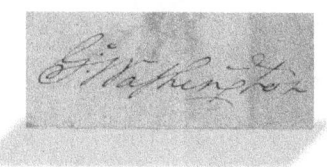

I'm still looking out the window between the taters and the sky is growing a darker green. Now, I don't know how many storms I've seen come this way over these mountains in the last 45 years but this one, this one is different.

The clouds just don't look right, and they have a pale green hue. They are tumbling and churning like I've never seen. The lightning is greenish and the thunder sounds more like a large growl.

To my knowledge no one has ever documented what happens when the Boouke shows up. Therefore, I am attempting to do that, so if, and when anyone does find this, they might know our story and our struggle and perhaps find a way to kill this evil that kills so many of us.

From the stories I've heard it does not distinguish between men and women, adults and children. There have been children left without parents and parents left without children. I ought to know, it took my parents the last time it arrived.

Wow, the wind is starting to pick up quite a bit now with still a pale green hue to the sky and air. Ooh, the smell! The only way I can describe it is that it is starting to smell like a decaying carcass and urine and it is getting stronger. It is really nauseating.

My wife and children are already hidden and I will not write down where they are just in case the Boouke is able to read and finds them. The potato hanging around my neck keeps getting in the way of my writing but is a small price to pay for possible safety, but who knows.

I have given my family strict instructions to remain perfectly quiet and still. No matter what happens I know they will follow my instructions. I can hear them, periodically crying and fearing for their lives, and mine. I feel so sorry for them and now I know how my real Pa felt when I was just five and it came to our community, utter helplessness.

I am writing as fast as I can because we don't know, according to past oral history, when the growling and screaming will start. Who will be the first? Last? All of us? Some? Me? My family?

I am trying to keep my head focused on writing so the fear will not overtake me. It's hard to keep my hand steady. True fear does weird things to a person. Makes him think and do things he wouldn't normally do with rational thoughts and sound mind.

With my family hid, the Bible to my left, my notebook in front and my shotgun on my right I feel as prepared as I could be against a predator no one has ever seen and lived to tell a convincing story of it. The rest of our community is hunkering down after Robert Lee rang the "Boouke Bell." We have had drills once a month for the last forty some odd years. Today the bell rang for real. We all knew what to do. So, here we are. It's real, too real.

All we can do is sit and wait for the worst to happen in child-like helplessness. As I sit here, waiting for what my Pa called a "Massacre of eradication" to pour out it's damnable fury, I might as well share the other memories I have of conversations about the Boouke I've had over the years. I did not mention the Boouke for two years after that conversation with Pa.

Then, two years later when I was sixteen I started getting sick so I went to see Doc. Strangely enough, there is not much sickness in our community. No new people to come in bringing new infections and we all eat pretty healthy. There is the occasional cold or stomach ache, ear ache but nothing too major. So, I went to see Doc because of a cold and sore throat. After he gave me my medicine, I stopped at the door before leaving, turned around and asked Doc a question.

"Doc, can you tell me what you know about the Boouke?"

His back was turned toward me and he was sorting papers. He stopped dead still and without turning around he said in a slightly angry and frustrated voice,

"Listen, you will rarely hear me say this but there are some things that even doctors don't know about. It's in your best interest that you run along now. I have things I have to tend to."

I said, "But my Pa said I am allowed to talk to any man in our community now about these things."

Without turning around to address me, Doc retorted, "Yes, that is true, but that doesn't mean that *any* man wants to talk to *you* about those things and I don't. So, I am politely asking you to move on along now, take your medicine as I have prescribed and have a good day, lad. I have things I need to tend to."

I stood there and stared at him for a few seconds and he never turned around, as I'm sure he hasn't heard the door shut yet. I walked out and never said anything to Doc again about the Boouke.

Oh! There is that foul stench blowing through again! Oh goodness it's almost too much to breathe as it sweeps through and stays. Again, like a smell of ammonia, stale urine and a hint of a dead carcass. I don't know if that means the Boouke is close or if this is just part of the arrival. My heart is beating out of my chest and it's hard to breath because of the fear. I, we, can do nothing about it.

OOOH! A huge noise behind the house like a tree blew over. I continue to sit in silence to see if I can hear footsteps, a growl or a door open. Nothing. Just a tree I reckon blowing over in the wind.

Ahhh! A shadow just passed in front of the window! I ran and checked on the family talking to each one of them assuring them that we are safe and that they are ok. They are scared but assured me they're fine. They begged me to be in with them, but I told them I need to be out here to protect them and to document this so that others might not have to go through it. I assured them I'd be in there at the proper time.

After Doc would not listen to me or answer my questions, I waited another year before I talked to Adam, our Gardner. Adam was a strong man but with a gentle soul and kind personality. One afternoon while Adam was taking a break I asked him if I could ask him a personal question.

"Sure!" He said with a smile.

"Could we step inside your house and lock the door first?" I countered?

"Oh, I see," he said. "Let's go."

Inside he invited me to sit down. When Adam moved here he brought with him a very comfortable cushy chair that I loved to sit in.

"Adam, I love this chair, where did you get it?"

He started laughing. "Well, there is a long story about that chair, it's very old. Would you like to hear the story?"

"Yes sir!" I said.

He sat down, leaned forward and put his elbows on his knees and clasped his hands together. "The story of this chair started back around 1760. My third great-grandfather, Stephen Alcott was a furniture builder in New York. He was commissioned by none other than George Washington to build him a set of furniture with a desk, so he did. He personally delivered it to Washington himself in Philadelphia where Mr. Washington used it to entertain dignitaries from France, Spain and many other places around the world, not to mention all our founding fathers.

When George Washington died in 1799, they kept much of his belongings, and some of his stuff was stolen. However, there was one chair left from the set my ancestor made him. So, my third- great-grandfather who made it, was contacted to see if he would like it back? At first, he said they could keep it but then he reconsidered and thought it would be nice to have a piece of his own furniture that our first President commissioned and owned so he accepted it back. Over the years it was protected and it was refinished and handed down to the oldest Alcott boy until it got to me. When I agreed to come live at Three Rivers, I didn't care what I had to leave behind as long as I could bring this chair. It was a pain to pack up but we got it here and now, you are sitting in *the* chair that George Washington owned and sat in himself! What do you think about that?"

My eyes were as big as saucers. I said, "I don't feel like I even deserve to sit in this chair!"

Adam smiled, "I know exactly how you feel. But Mr. Washington was a man of the people and he would be delighted for you to sit in his chair. So, enjoy it."

I sat there in silence for a moment rubbing the arms looking at the claw feet and the decorative wood.

I asked, "So this chair was in the Presidential Mansion?"

"Well, yes and no," he said. "The Official Presidential Mansion wasn't finished until 1800 and John Adams was the first President to live in it. In fact, Will, if this chair was there, there is a good chance that it would not be here today."

"Why?" I asked in confusion.

"Because the British invaded America again in 1812 and they burned the Presidential Mansion down in 1814 and this chair would have been burned up. When my ancestor decided he wanted it back, that saved the chair forever!"

"Wow!" I can't believe this chair has such a great history!"

"Where did George Washington live as President if the Official Presidential Mansion wasn't built?" I was quickly becoming a history lover and student.

"Great question. Washington's first place to live as President was the Osgood Mansion in New York City. All the places the Presidents lived were called the Presidential Mansions. In Philadelphia Mr. Washington lived in the

Masters' Mansion and it was called the President's House. George Washington lived there from 1790 to 1797. Do you know what else is special about this chair?"

"No, tell me!" I couldn't wait to hear.

George himself, sat right in this chair and wrote his memories of the American Revolution. You can't get any more historical than this chair!"

I was so engrossed in the history and the past that I forgot where I was and why I was even there to talk to Adam. I was day dreaming about the chair, and not saying a word.

Adam broke the silence and said, "Well. . . I think you had something to ask me?"

"Oh!" I said, drawing me out of the wonderful history of the past. "Sorry, actually what I wanted to talk to you about just doesn't compare to what you were describing in this chair. But the question I had was this, I'd like to know what you know about the Boouke?"

"Well, you were too young to remember, that after what the community called the 'Massacre of eradication' happened about 40 years ago, most people here were taken or eaten, or just disappeared. Gone. We don't know what happened to them. The community needs nine families to sustain it. Your Pa took a trip back to town and quietly talked to several people to recruit families for the support and continuation of the Three Rivers community. He talked to me, I heard everything he said and considered my options. I decided to come back with your Pa and live the rest of my life here at Three Rivers. With Mr. Washington's chair of course."

"Why did you decide to come?" I asked.

"Because as the poet Thoreau said, '*I went to the woods because I decided to live deliberately.*' I wanted something more than what I was living. I wanted a challenge and community. So, I decided to come. Boy, your Pa was so excited. We gathered up a bunch of vitals, supplies and so forth and headed out. I haven't regretted it a day since being here. I say I haven't regretted it, but I haven't experienced the Boouke yet either."

In a quieter tone I asked timidly, "Did Pa explain to you about the Boouke before you came??"

"Yes, as much as he knew."

"And you decided to come anyway? Why?" I really wanted to know.

Adam looked me right in the eye and said, "Will, you only get one go around in life. If you never did things because of the possibility of failure or fear or forfeiture, then you wouldn't do anything. If you live like that, life is not worth living. It's better to try and fail than to never try at all. You see Will, it's my reckoning that those who never try and follow their dreams, never know the satisfaction of victory and accomplishment. Yes, your Pa explained the Boouke very clearly to me, as much as he knew, and told me if I had any doubt at all, not to come and that he would understand. Well, I decided to come and it has been worth it.

"Now, Will, I've never experienced the Boouke myself and hope not to, but I certainly have heard stories after I got here. I probably can't tell you any more than what you've already heard but it's a terrible evil with no known way to kill it. Wait, Joe Dilly did tell me one story that I just now remembered. He said that he doesn't like to talk about it but he'd share this with me only once and never talk about it again. He said when the whole thing was going down that night, he thought he got a glimpse of it through the cracks between the boards in the potato cellar."

I jumped in, "What did it look like? Did he say?!" Adam continued, "All Joe said was it kind of looked like a huge dark man, almost hairy like walking in a shadowy fog or something then all of a sudden it was down on all fours like a creature he'd never seen. Then it just disappeared."

"It changed from a man to a creature?" I asked with excitement.

"I didn't say that. I'm just telling you what Joe Dilly thought he saw."

Still excited I asked, "Was he pretty sure that's what he saw?"

"Here's what I know Will, he was so sure that he saw it and it scared him so bad that he told me he would never talk about it again. You know Joe, you can't get him to shut up when he's talking. For him to refuse to talk about something, well, in my book I'd say that's the real deal. But I wouldn't go ask him about it if I was you. Just take the story from me and let him have his peace."

"I'll not mention it to him. Thank you, Adam. I'll keep all this to myself."

"Oh, Will, one more thing. As you know I am a lover of poetry. I am going to quote you one more saying by Thoreau then I want to give you a gift."

"A gift? You don't have to do that!"

"I want to. Will, this is the quote that drove me here and I want it to be the one that drives you to your dreams, whatever those may be. Here is Thoreau's quote, *"Most men live lives of quiet desperation and go to their grave with the song still in them."* I didn't want to come to the end of my life with my song still in me and I hope you don't either. Wait right here."

He got up, walked through the taters hanging down over the doorway and went to the back room. He was gone for two or three minutes and came back with a book. I'm sure my eyes got wide.

"Will, I want to give you this book. It's yours, you don't have to give it back. I've written a little inscription in the front for you from me but don't read it until you get home. And Will, what I wrote in there I meant! Please accept it."

I was a bit confused but said, "Yes sir."

Adam continued, "Now back to the book itself, I hope you read it with interest, knowledge and excitement. It has got me through many a mid-night drearies while I pondered weak and weary.

"What does that mean?" I was confused again.

He smiled and chuckled. "In this book, I want you to find a poem about a bird and read it. Then read it again and then a third time and think about it. Then read the other stories in there but read them slowly and deliberately. When you do, you'll dream dreams that no mortal has ever dared to dream before."

Excitedly I asked, "Is that in there too?"

"Yes. You'll come across it."

My heart was overjoyed from receiving this book. I had never heard of Edgar Allen Poe. That's when I also fell in love with poetry and writing. I guess it's ironic that I am writing this 'horror story' as it is really happening. I'm sure Poe could have written it much better of course. No, I wouldn't have wanted him to live through this either. After he gave me the book I looked at him after opening the door to leave and said, "Oh, Adam?"

"Yes."

"Keep your taters up."

"HAHA! You too, Will. You too. Enjoy the book. It will give you a lifetime of pleasure. Remember, find the story about a bird, and, what I wrote in the front, I mean it."

I nodded with a smile and we dismissed our meeting. I wanted to look in the front so bad to see what he wrote but he told me to wait until I got home and that's what I did. I ran through the front door so fast Ma didn't have a chance to say a word. Running through the taters hanging down in front of my door I jumped on my bed and looked at the front of the book. Nervously, I opened the front cover and there was Adams writing.

"Dear Will, I hope that this book inspires you through your lifetime as much as it did me. Read it carefully and with thoughtful adventure.

Now, I have never seen anyone so passionate as I am about Mr. Washington's chair. I could tell you were in awe and mesmerized by it. Your deep respect for this chair told me that you are to have it. I have enjoyed it for many, many years and I would have no better joy and pleasure than to be able to pass it on to you. I mean this. Don't argue! I would like one last week with George's chair then next week I would like for you to come and get it. I will write down the history of the chair and give you that as well. I am so happy to know your excitement! Treat it well, respect it deeply and use it freely. George would be proud!

Your Friend,

Adam Alcott   August 9, 1900

Yes, that actually happened. As you might guess, I am sitting in Mr. Washington's chair as I write, with deep gratitude toward Adam and awe for this piece of furniture. When I die today, as most likely we all will, I will have had a good life with a wonderful family and this chair as a beautiful gift.

After that conversation with Adam, we went back to living our normal lives and I have devoured that book's poems and 'Many a quaint and curious story of forgotten lore' many times over in that wonderful chair. Those two items were the most precious gift that I believe I have ever received from someone.

Years went by with small conversations about the Boouke here and there. As time passed I had a few young boys come to me and ask the same questions I had asked our Elders when I was young. They pretty much got the same answers. However, I never gave them my Poe or my chair.

Chapter 12

The First Wave

As I continue to look out of the window nothing much has changed in the last few minutes. It may be getting a little darker and greener hue outside. My heart beat and anxiety eases up a little when I am writing about my memories. However, when I stop writing and think about this moment and the present danger we all know is coming, I feel my heart beating so hard it hurts every time it pumps in my chest.

"What is that?" I pondered out loud looking out my window at the sky toward Megan's Hill. "What?" There are lights, white lights that look like flash lights going across the face of the mountain but there is certainly nobody over there! No one lives within forty miles of here. There they go again! They go across then stop then go and change direction either going down or up and then they just disappear!

There they are again! What is that? One then two then none. Oh boy, I'm getting scared. Too fast for a person if it was a person but it's not. Traveling the face of the mountain. It looks like flying lights, but it can't be!

Oh! Wait. I just heard a voice!

"William!?"

"Yes?" I yelled.

"Are you ok?"

"Yep. You?"

"Hunkered down!"

"Keep your taters up Robert!"

"You too!"

It was Robert Lee, the old man of our group, checking on everyone. Right now, everyone answered. That's a good sign so far.

Wow! Those lights continue to travel across the mountain! This lightning and thunder is just weird. I mean I've never seen. . .

OH NO! Something just pounded on my front door! Three solid knocks! One right after the other in sequence! Was it debris from the wind? I'm holding my breath. Just listening. Nothing more. No footsteps. Must have been debris. Yes, that's what I'll assume it was, only debris and nothing more.

Well, I've sat here for thirty minutes just staring outside at the strange lights and praying while the wind is getting stronger. "Lord, we really need Your help about now." My children are not old enough to know about the Boouke. Yet, when I was little I had no concept about. . .

What the. . .? Three more distinct knocks on my front door. That's not debris! Oh no! There they go again! Three pounding knocks. OK Will, get ahold of yourself. I know that no one is out of their house. We've gone over this in drills once a week the last forty years. No one leaves till the bell rings "All clear."

Who or *what is* that?

"William are you in there?"

Oh, my goodness it is a female voice from outside!

"William, this is Catheryn, Joshua's wife. I got lost. Can I come in?"

This is too weird! Why would Catheryn come to my house instead of hers? They just live to the left of us! I said nothing. That was the drill.

Another voice from across the way yelled, "William?"

It was Shelby.

"Yes!" I yelled over the wind.

"Are you at my front door?"

"NO!!"

"Somebody sayin' he's you and he's wantin' in!"

"Don't do it Shelby! I'm in my house!"

Shelby yelled back, "What's going on will? What's happening? If it's not you then who is it?

"I don't know Shelby! I'm hearing Catheryn's voice outside my door."

Joshua yells back, "Catheryn is in here with me!"

I yell back, "It must be part of the deception. Keep your taters up!"

"Ok. You too!"

Silence. No knocking. No voices. Ut oh. Wow! The wind just went dead still. Okay, this is not normal. Keep your head William, keep calm. Hmmm. Why did I hear Catheryn's voice at my door and Shelby heard mine at his door? Was *someone* really there? This is just too strange.

All the potatoes around every house are dead still and hanging straight down. There they were every one of them absolutely still with no movement. What is going on?

Minutes are passing so slowly. There is no stir or sound outside. No crickets chirping, no birds singing or flying, no frogs croaking, only dead silence.
I wonder what. . .

Oh no! Voices right outside my window. Woa! There's the shadow that just went past the window again! Oh! Another shadow past the other window, huge! This time it stopped! Uhhh. . . it is bending down and looking in. Turning its large hairy looking head left then right, its trying to see! Oh no! Now they are surrounding us! The voices! They sound like they are talking but in low muttering sounds, grunts and clicking. I can't make out anything they are saying nor, can I see any distinct physical bodies. What!? Now I hear them in our bedroom! How can that be?!?! I ran in there with my shotgun but no voices! No one was there. I slowly walked back to my desk at the window shotgun in hand. I can hardly breathe and I'm starting to cough from the stench outside. I'm going crazy! Ok, Will, keep your head. You're ok. Breathe. I began to talk out loud, "George? Is this the anxiety you felt at Valley Forge?"

Woa! There was a big strike of green lightning and now the growling thunder. I'm telling you this waiting is terror!

Shelby yelled back again, "William!"

"Yes Shelby."

"I'm hearin' voices outside. You see anybody out my way?"

I got up and cautiously went to the window to look out. Our houses were built so that we all have a clear view of the front porches of all the other houses.

"No!" I shouted back through the window. "But I heard them too."

Another voice from the community yelled out, "Yep, me too." And another, "I second that!"

"Good" Shelby yelled, "I'm not crazy!"

Robert Lee shouted out, "We can decide that in council meeting!" There was laughs all around. That helped to ease the tension for just a moment. I fear that if these records remain, I might be thought a mad man, writing such happenings. I am of sound mind and body and want the world to be rid of this evil. If there is anything. . .

Oh, dear Father! Help us! There it is! "Oh God of our fathers please be our shelter and shield! Please help us during our hour of tribulation."

Aah! There is the growl! A low long drawn out deep guttural growl with a heavy breath on the end. "Dear God, we need Your help. We must be delivered from this inexplicable terror!" A second growl. This time it was a little further away moving toward Dane's house. I dare not holler at him for fear of attracting the Boouke back to my house. Oh, that sounds so terrible! But I must protect my wife and kids and Dane his.

Dane is the guy that keeps the community at ease. Jolly and very cordial and polite, everyone likes Dane. He always finds something funny in some situation or has a story to tell or it reminds him of something else and it ends up so funny you just have to laugh! I'll never forget the story he made up about my Pa and Shelby. One day at Community Council meeting when the meeting was over, Robert asked if anyone else had anything to say. It got quiet and Dane spoke up and said, "I'd like to share a story before we go."

Robert said, "Ok, Dane you have the floor."

Dane said, "I heard through the grapevine that a few years ago, Pete and Shelby went to town to get some supplies. While at the dry goods store they decided to get in on the weekly charity raffle at the last minute. They each bought one ticket for a dollar.

The raffle was for six prizes they were drawing for in fifteen minutes so Pete and Shelby 'cided they were going to stay and see if they won anything. The first five prizes were drawn and neither of them won a thing. But when the sixth prize was drawn it was Pete's ticket number! He won the brand-new toilet brush!

The two then made their way back to Two Rivers and when they got back they didn't really say anything about the raffle because they thought some people might think that's gambling so they kept it quiet. About a week or so had passed when the men were talking one day, and Shelby said,

"Say Pete, how did you like your prize you won, that new toilet brush?"

To which Pete replied, "Not so good, I'm thinking 'bout switching back to paper."

That brought the house down! For months after that people would carry little pieces of toilet paper in their pockets and offer it to my Pa at various and sundry times. My Pa took it well and in stride. Dane was a Joker! However, if you ever got him mad... get out of his way and don't say a word because when he flies off the handle; Well, no one can handle him until he calms down. As a logger, he just doesn't know his own strength. Not only is he the funniest, but he is the largest and strongest man in our community.

Dane stands about six foot four inches and weighs about 210. He has thick sandy blond hair and boy can he sing! He's got a set of pipes on him like nobody's business. Robert calls him 'the man with the golden voice.' He's always singing something and whatever it is, it is good. Sometimes, he entertains us with three or four songs in a row when it gets late and we have nothing to do. I love to hear him sing, "Oh, Danny Boy." I tear up every time he sings it. He sure has a voice. We call him 'Singin' Dane."

There's the growl again.

I yelled out "PA!!"

No answer.

"PA!!!"

"Yep?"

"You and Ma ok?"

"Hunkered tight!"

"OK Pa. Keep your taters up!"

"You too Will. Remember Will, the Word of God will help you through evil times!"

"Got it Pa. Thanks."

No screams yet from anyone in the community. That's a good sign. The only thing I can think of is that the wind must have died down so it could get a good location on our scent. But how powerful is this thing that it controls the wind? "God, please let those potatoes work."

"AAAAAHHH!!!" Another pounding on my door!

"William, it's Catheryn. Please! Come to the door and let me in. Please, I'm begging you!"

I said nothing. I am not moving. My heart is pounding in my throat. Am I really hearing this voice or am I going Mad? NO! I heard it. Shelby and others heard it.

"Ok, ok Will. Stop. Think. Reason. Breathe." Alright, I feel a little better. Reason is returning to my mind.

Oh no! Pounding again at my door! Should I get my shotgun and shoot through the door? Then, what if I give it an opening to come in? But what if I kill it and rid us all of this evil terror. What if I shoot it and the pellets do nothing? How Many in the past have shot it in my same hopes and yet died at the mercy of the Boouke because it can't be killed? What to do? I don't know what to do! I just can't sit here!

Out of nowhere something hit the door with such a force, I jumped out of my chair and dropped my pen and shotgun. Whatever that thing is, it just got angry and slammed the door yelling, "AAAAHHHH!!"

I scrambled to get my gun and sat with my back to the opposite wall facing the front door ready to shoot if anything busts in. I am trembling so hard, I doubt if anyone can read my writing right now. Here I sit. A prisoner in my own home. Forty years ago, my parents were so fearful for me. They protected me and threw me in the potato cellar. Now I am responsible for my family and I can't, I cannot let them be taken or eaten by the Boouke. Oh, my goodness! The shadow just passed in front of the window. Wait, it stopped, it's still there but I can't make it out. Just a shadow. I'm sure it must be trying to look in. There it goes past the window. Can it see in side or does it feel my fear? If it feeds on my fear, then its belly must be full!

Chapter 13

Psychological Warfare

I hear footsteps all around the house. A few steps and it stops. A few more steps and it stops. Oh, there was another shadow passing by the window! A huge shadow of what looked like a big hairy man! It has stopped right behind the house right now between the two back windows. I can see nothing. For a few minutes it has not moved. It's hiding between the two windows so that I cannot see it. What do I do? This will be sure death at the hands of pure evil. I know that it is wanting in.

What does this thing know? Does it know that it is terrifying us, or does it just do its thing and our terror is the by-product of its nature? Is it intentionally stalking or truly thinking the best way to get to us? I just thought of something, why doesn't it just break down the door or break through a window? Maybe it is because we have the potatoes tied up there. I feel that this thing is going to get bold and start tearing into every house and eat us all alive, or whatever it does with its prey. Something must be done.

All of a sudden, as if by the tide of the ocean my soul was consumed with the deepest fear and darkest terror and depression, I knew what I had to do. I know what must be done. It would be far better for my family to die at *my* will with my shotgun and then myself rather than to succumb to the rotten foulness of this demon. There I said it. In mercy, I must kill my family. I heard the voices in my head saying, "*Do it.*"

I walked to the cellar under the floor in the back bedroom. "God, please forgive me for what I am about to do." I knelt down and slid the rug to the side that was covering the opening. I put my finger in the lid hole and pulled open the door leaning it all the way back on the floor. Kneeling, I looked into the eyes of my wife and two little children. In my mind I silently prayed, "God You know my heart. May You have mercy on my soul."

"*Do it.*" I pulled back the left hammer of my double-barrel shotgun, "God You know my heart's pure motive. This has to be done." "*Do it.*" Then I pulled back the right hammer. I hadn't yet raised the gun in the presence of the family. They don't know what must be done or what is coming but it will be quick and painless and merciful. "*Do it.*" What I am about to do is way more loving than letting them be eaten or taken or whatever happens to them by the Boouke. "*Yes, that's right. You can do it. It's more merciful. Do it.*"

Immediately tears began to flow from my eyes. Through stammered crying I managed to get out what I wanted to say. "*Do it now.*"

"Martha, my dear wife. I love you. James, Madison my two sweet kids. You are the light of my life. I couldn't imagine anything happening to you out of my control."

"*Go ahead, do it.*" Martha, through her tears said, "I love you Will. Thank you for protecting us."

"I love you too daddy!" My children said through their crying tears. "*Shoot them! Kill them!*" They were hunkered down there with their arms about the other one, in a loving hug. "*Do it!*"

For some many minutes after this idea possessed me, we just kept looking at each other. I knelt motionless. Why couldn't I move? Why couldn't I gain the courage to save my family from a fate worse than death by allowing the Boouke to take them?

I began to tremble harder. I dared not make the effort to pull the trigger and seal our fate and yet there was something in my wretched mind that kept whispering an audible,

". . .*DO IT! DO IT NOW! SHOOT THEM!*"

I looked at my family and said, "I'm sorry."

I got up and grabbed the lid that covered the cellar opening and I closed the door over them taking the last look at my family. I brought the gun into place and secured it against my shoulder. *"Do it."* I eased the barrel down against the wood lid toward my wife first. *"SHOOT THEM!"* I put my finger on the trigger of that old shotgun and began to squeeze. *"NOW!"* The hammer fell with a click as I gently let it down without explosion. I did the same to the other hammer. I sat there in utter disbelief thinking about what I was going to do. The family was none the wiser to my potentially wicked plan. I felt so ashamed and relieved at the same time.

Immediately I heard a demonic yell outside that said, *"NO! I said, 'shoot them!"*

What? Was that in my head? Can it see inside but not get in? Can it control my thoughts? What is this thing we are dealing with? I ran back to my desk in a daze and sat down. With a deep breath, I knew I had recovered from this hellish influence. I had recovered the full use of my faculties. Again, Poe said, *"There are moments when, even to the sober eye of reason, the world of our sad humanity assumes the semblance of hell."* It sure did for me, for a brief moment.

Uhhh! There it is again! Three distinct knocks on my front door.

"Will, it's Martha, your wife. You said 'you were sorry' so I came outside to see if we were in danger and the door shut behind me. Unlock the door and let me in!"

What?! Yes, that was *her* voice! I ran to the cellar and yanked opened the door. There were the two kids but no Martha! What?

"Where is your mother!?!" I was screaming. "Where is your mother? Where is she! Tell me!"

"In the bathroom daddy." They were bawling hysterically. I ran to the bathroom screaming "Martha, you in there?" I grabbed the door and pulled it open. She was just getting up.

"Yes?" She said curiously.

"You tell me *anytime* you leave the cellar! Were you just outside?"

A look of terror and confusion came over her, "Heavens no!"

"Get in the cellar!" I was more relieved than scared, but I was not mad at her.

"What's wrong Will? I just had to go."

155

"Look Martha, you're not going to believe this but I just heard *your* voice outside on the porch saying it was you and for me to let you in."

She raised her hand to her mouth and gasped in terror. "Will, it wasn't me, I promise. . ."

Putting my arm around her and drawing her as close to me as I could, I whispered, "I know Martha it just scared me that's all." "How did it know I said, 'I'm sorry' to you a moment ago?"

Confused Martha said, "What?"

"Your voice...uh...*the* voice acting like you said, 'Will, you said you were sorry so I came outside to see what was wrong.' How did it know I said that?"

"Oh my, Will! Does it hear all we say?"

"I don't know." I began to whisper very softly, "Listen, just go back to the cellar with the kids and comfort them." I gave her a loving kiss and we stood there for a moment both knowing the obvious outcome to the end of the day, but we dare not speak about it, especially when it came to the kids. That, you just don't think about.

I was immediately setting at my desk without any recollection of walking in there and sitting down. I have so much adrenalin, my head is spinning.

"Let me in!!! Aaaargh!"

It spoke English! But I just realized it did a moment ago too when it yelled 'I told you to shoot!' It speaks! What are we dealing with? This deep voice from hell yelled so loud it literally rattled the windows. Was this thing making the voices we heard outside our houses? Wait! What did Pa say? I just remembered! "The Word of God will help you through evil times!" Well, it's worth a try.

"God, please provide me a sword when I need it. May Your Word be a sword." I grabbed the Bible and cautiously moved toward the door, although I still had my shotgun ready. I eased very quietly across the room and placed the Bible against the door.

"Noooooooooo!"

It yelled with a tremendous force and I heard it run off a good twenty yards or so. It worked! The thing sounded like a horse running on all fours. It worked! The Word of God sent away evil! Wow! But, what is this thing? Is there only one of these things? More? Inside everyone else's brain are we all perceiving the same thing? Different? Does it go from house to house?

Oh no. There is that same long drawn out growl again on the other side of the square.

"Oh, Dear God no!" There was the first scream from someone in our community, but I couldn't make out the voice. The scream continued, "No! No! Don't take me! I could hear some scuffle and struggle. The growling of wild rabid evil! Tortured scream of horrible pain! Oh, I can't take this. It could have been me or my family! "Dear God, please make it go away!"

I had to listen and, in a sense, "stay" to the end for support with the one who was about to be gone even though they didn't know it. I was rooting for them, but they kept screaming!

"Elsie! Boys! I love you! No!! I won't . . ."

Silence. No more screaming. No growling. Complete silence. Dear Lord, how much more of this can this little community take? Why God, why? It was Doc Carl, in his unprotected home. Poor boys. Randy and Matt must have heard that and they are left with the last thing they heard from their father, screams of horror. They are orphans now. I can't imagine what they are going through.

It's so quiet. I wonder if it is stalking another home or person. I don't hear footsteps. Eerie quietness. I don't want to be to laborious with Poe but the silence reminds me of the end of his sonnet that says something like this,

"The corporate Silence: dread him not!

No power hath he of evil in himself;

But should some urgent fate

Bring me to meet his shadow

That haunted the lone regions

where no foot of man has trod,

commend thyself to God!"

That's exactly what I've been trying to do,
commending myself to God. Thanks Edgar for the
reminder.

Chapter 14

The wind picks up

Deep into the darkness peering out the window with trepidation, it seems the wind is starting to pick up again a bit. Does that mean it's gone? For a while? For good? Or just time to devour its first people flesh then it comes back for more? I can't take much more, but we must endure.

Oh no! The door! Three more knocks!

"Will, this is Robert Lee. I ran over here while it's gone. Let me in and we'll formulate a plan."

I sat there in even more fear, if that was possible, not knowing what is real anymore. I glanced out the side window through the taters and it was Robert Lee at my door. I ran to the door and grabbed the handle to open it.

I yelled out, "Robert Lee!?!"

"Yes Will, I'm outside."

I know this is not in our plans, but he is *standing* outside my door! He is physically there! I was looking at him through the window!

Again, I called out, "Robert Lee!"

Again, he said from outside my door, "What Will, let me in?"

I questioned, "That story you told me yesterday. What was the name of the plow mule you had as a youngster? What was her name?"

Silence.

"You know it Robert, what was your mule's name?"

"Will her name was Sarah. She was my work mule when I was young."

"I backed away from the door. I knew that wasn't the right answer."

I yelled louder this time, "Robert Lee?!?!"

A voice came from across the way, "Yes Will, what is it?"

"Where are you now?"

"Will, we're hunkered down! WHY?"

"No reason. Keep your taters up!"

"OK. You too."

I did not go to the door. *Wham*!!!! This evil hit the door with more aggressive anger this time. Whatever this thing is, it appears to be able to shape shift or something into people or things and mimic them. It has intelligence and motive! Yes, I've answered my own question I pondered a moment ago. This thing knows it's terrorizing us. It's playing with us but we're not as easy prey as it thought we were going to be. But how do we fight it?

Oh Lord please help us! Another long deep drawn out growl. I'm looking through the window. Growling, constant growling. "Oh, please no." It looks like Robert standing on Joshua's porch knocking! "Joshua! NO!" I yelled through the window. He opened the door expecting to see Robert and, in a flash,, this thing transformed into something hideous and grabbed Joshua! The second scream in our community.

Joshua is screaming, "NO! NO! Help! Someone help m . . .
Again, silence. It got him. He ventured outside of the potatoes and it got him!

A third scream immediately followed. No!!! This time it was a child! "God have mercy!" It was Dane's boy, DJ. Joshua was his neighbor and DJ's favorite man of the community. Apparently when Joshua was yelling, DJ couldn't stand it and went outside to 'help' and immediately the Boouke snatched him up too.

DJ's screaming didn't last long. The Boouke grabbed him and was gone, just disappeared! I couldn't believe it! I continued looking outside toward his house. Dane ran outside yelling at the Boouke, through his hysterical tears, crying and yelling, "You demon from hell! Come back here and I'll kill you myself! Come back! Come baaaaaack! Bring my boy back! Come back here you demon from hell! I'll kill you!" Dane was impulsive like that. Who could blame him when his kid was taken. Perhaps I would do the same thing.

Outside under the trees, Dane was so broken with sorrow he just fell to his knees and sobbed alone in the grassy square.

I yelled, "Dane, get back! Get inside! Go! Go!"

Dane was so overwhelmed by sorrow he didn't even hear me. He just sat there. Suddenly the biggest man like creature covered with dark brown almost black hair appeared and stood in front of him. This creature was at least eight to nine feet tall. Dane jumped up quickly with his gun raised pointing upward to the creature's head.

"Who are you!" Dane yelled.

"The creature man just stood there in silence."

Delirious from sorrow, Dane pulled both hammers back on his shotgun and fired both barrels at once directly toward the creature's face at almost point-blank range. There was no way on earth he could miss.

As soon as the gun went off, the tall hairy creature man fell to the ground, transformed into some creature on all fours and pounced on Dane. It was so fast. In just a half a second Dane was on the ground fighting, doing what he could. If there was anyone in camp who could fight this thing, it was Dane. Dane was hitting, kicking, punching and he just avoided a swipe by the beast's paw and turned his head to the side to avoid the claws. As soon as his head was turned the beast lunged so quick that its long teeth sank top and bottom deep into his neck and quicker than lightening, the whole community heard Dane's neck go *SNAP*! It was so loud.

His throat and everything in his neck were instantly ripped out before he even had a chance to yell. It was that fast.

Chapter 15
The Boouke

"Oh, dear God! Please don't let this happen this way! No, please no…" I kept saying out loud. The creature somehow knew that I had been watching. With Dane still in his mouth by the throat, his body still quivering and jerking, it looked at me, squinted its yellow eyes with long vertical black slits for pupils and smiled. It dropped Dane to the ground and disregarded him as if he were a play toy.

Dane's body was still convulsing with energy. With every pump of his still beating heart, blood is squirting out with oxygen everywhere like a red bubbly foam fountain from his arteries. Horrific! He is trying to breathe and his mouth is moving but he only makes a gurgling sound through the thick blood filling up his mouth and running out. His fingers and feet are twitching uncontrollably. There are so many holes in his face. His neck entrails were stripped out and are hanging below his chin with the rest of his esophagus, muscles and tendons. The skin on half his face was ripped off up to the top of his skull and you can see his bloodstained pinkish white jawbone and cheekbone up to his empty eye socket. His right eye is hanging out of the dark round hole where it used to set, swinging on the thin nerve that was still attached somewhere in the back of his head. Blood is oozing out where his nose used to be and his lips were no longer there. His chest is rising and falling as if he were still determined to kill the beast. I only hope he is already dead, so he doesn't feel anything. Dane's chest just fell for the last time and no more white foam is bubbling out from his mouth. The blood has stopped squirting and now only spreading on the ground looking like a red lake. Poor man. He died for his child. Commendable.

The beast slowly turned, taking very light deliberate steps until it faced me, and we were staring into each other's eyes through my window. I was shaking so hard it was like I was having seizures. It walked extremely slow taking thought of every step very intently and quietly with its head lowered and its shoulder blades rising high above its neck and head. It was smiling, intentionally smiling at me with Dane's blood still dripping off the long teeth. Straight toward my house it came never taking its gaze off mine. It walked as if for an eternity and stopped about ten yards in front of my porch. "Oh, dear Father, please help me."

It just sat there. A creature no human eyes should have to stare into. Unadulterated evil in its purest form. A smooth skinned creature with no hair anywhere on its body. It walked on all fours and its back legs bent like a horse's legs. When it stopped walking it crouched and sat up on its hind quarters, squatting with its front paws swinging slowly left and right in the air as if to hypnotize those watching.

It had no nose, just a single hole. Its mouth was larger than it looked like it should be. A long narrow slit cut side to side with teeth protruding outward both from the top down and from the bottom up. It looked through the tops of its big round yellow eyes with the black slit pupils set deep under its large brow. It just sat there. Its brow as it were was raising and lowering slightly and it would tilt its head trying to figure me or the situation out. It has intelligence and the ability to formulate a plan. Every so often it would glance left and right as if to keep in mind what was around.

After a long while its brow began to lower and stay there with an evil look, then, it began to growl that long slow drawn out growl that we'd heard three times earlier.

"Well," I said out loud, "I guess it's my turn." It kept growling the lowest most evil guttural growl that human ears have ever heard. It made my soul melt like wax. It just sat there growling. Long and slow. Looking at me. Sizing me up as if I were some formidable foe. Ha.

It continued to growl. Very still. The muscles under its pale green smooth skin were twitching and undulating back and forth in excitement and anticipation of a quick attack and kill.

Martha yelled, "Will I heard it growling!"

I never took my gaze off this hellish imp. "Martha! Stay in the cellar!"

"Will, are you ok?"

"Stay in the cellar!!" It began to crouch lower, ever so slowly with a demonic smile of what it was about to do.

Here I am. Staring into the eyes of evil personified. Sizing it up and it knows it. A grimacing scowl came across its face. I thought to myself, "I wonder. . .

IT LEAPS!

I jumped back in the room away from the window!

But the beast only jumped a few feet and stopped! Why? What was it up to? Is it feeling my fear? Tormenting me? Playing with me? Judging my reaction?

Suddenly, from who knows where and why, I felt courage rise within me. What is this? I. . .am going to take on this monster from hell? ME? It's as if I know the outcome, yes, my demise but this is what I must do. What is this surge of courage that has overcome me? I fear, yet I don't fear! This is the hour I thought. My hour. I walked to the door and opened it. I stepped out on the front porch with my gun raised, even closer to the beast now. I stared at the beast with a stare of death as much as I could muster and said, "No power of hell is going to defeat me today!" My heart became full!

I was quickly aware and perceived that this was personal! It didn't get me when I was little but it doesn't want me, it wants my children. How do I know this? Is it talking to me in my mind? I said in a calm but firm voice, not knowing if it could hear me or not:

"You're not getting my children. You will die first." It began to growl and growl.

I continued, "The fact is Boouke, if you were as powerful and evil as you claim to be I would not have gotten away the first-time. You're mistake years ago, will lead to your demise today. It began to back up. Growling it's long slow drawn out hellistic growl.

It backed up another five yards and just squatted there as if it was wondering what it was going to do or was supposed to do. Joshua and Carl were dead along with Dane's boy. Dane's body lay in the square with his throat hanging open in what looked like a lake of blood. The creature just sat there for a good ten minutes swaying back and forth looking directly at me. Waiting for the right and proper time to pounce upon me for another meal. His front legs, swaying back and forth, back and forth, back and forth.

Chapter 16
The Decision

From the corner of my eye I saw Robert Lee walk out of his house with his gun in hand pointed toward the Boouke. It turned toward Robert. Joe Dilly came out with his gun. The creature quickly turned again. Shelby, Adam and Pa all showed up with their guns raised at the beast. It was now turning circles growling. It was caught!

Apparently while I was talking to the beast, the men were yelling back and forth making plans while I had it distracted and occupied. The Boouke kept turning and turning in circles not knowing what to do.

It stopped circling. It ignored the other men somehow knowing they could not hurt it and it just looked at me and smiled. It seemed like an eternity! Nothing happened; time just stood still. The Boouke looked at me and began to communicate with me in my mind.

It said, *"I will eat you, your children and slowly devour your mate while she is still alive. It will be delicious."*

I don't know what came over me but I put my gun on the porch and stood there. I raised my arms out to the side and stood there with no weapon and helpless and said out loud, "Boouke, first you'll have to get through me." It began to laugh and laugh and without hesitation it leaped again so fast with such a jump toward me that all the men shot at it at the same time. It was hit but stayed very much alive!

Immediately I found myself underneath this hound from hell fighting for my life! Dodging claws, swipes and lunges with its protruding teeth. Green saliva was dripping from its teeth mixing with the dirt as we rolled along the ground. Its mouth was watering for people flesh. With green goo falling into my mouth and face I was gagging and blowing it back on the Boouke. I was almost drowning in this green putrid drippy liquid. Hardly being able to breathe and fighting with all I had, I could somehow feel myself being ripped here and there but there was so much adrenalin that it didn't hurt that bad!

All I knew was that I wasn't dead yet! Again, I felt courage fill my soul! I grabbed it by the neck and began to squeeze and choke it. It started to wheeze and cough. With one swipe of its claws it ripped into my forearm and dislodged my arm from its neck. As my arm hit the porch it landed on a stick. It was my son's 'monster sword,' he plays with. He dropped it there when I grabbed him to throw him into the potato cellar with Martha and Madison.

172

In one move I grabbed the 'sword' and swung it around and with all my might and strength I brought it right up to its eye and with an extra hard push I gouged "the monster sword" deep into the eye socket of the Boouke, pushing and rotating the stick in a circle feeling resistance as it hit bone. With only an ounce of strength left in my torn ripped muscles, I mustered up a final push and I felt the monster stick break through bone and cartilage and protrude another six inches as it easily went deeper into its green head covered with its own blood mingled with mine. I kept pushing and turning and rotating the stick pulsating it back and forth as it didn't want to let me go but had to because of the pain.

I heard one of the men yell, "Did you see that?"

Robert yelled, "Git 'em Will!"

As the Boouke backed off, I laid there in exhaustion, blood pouring out of my whole body, hurting and stinging and hardly able to move or breathe. I did my best to roll over toward the beast, so I could get a look at it before it pounced on me for the last time and got me for good.

What I saw next, I would NOT have believed if I had not seen it myself! It somehow transformed into a form of a huge man like creature covered with dark hair! It stood right up. It grabbed the stick with both hands and began to pull the 'sword' out of its head. It had trouble as it was buried so deeply. It turned and twisted the stick until it slid out with goo and blood making a slurping sound from the vacuum of the skin around it. It turned, looked at me and yelled as loud as anything we have ever heard. Quicker than lightning, it began to run so fast right at me and then in the middle of a giant leap it transformed into the beast again and just as I was rolling over to get up and out of its way, it was on top of me for the last time.

By now the men were reloaded but couldn't shoot because they would hit me. I grabbed both its paws and with its mouth wide open and green slick saliva dripping in my eyes and nose, it came straight down for my neck. "CRACK!" It hit the wooden boards of the porch as I let go just at the right time and rolled to the side.

At that moment I heard Pa yell, "Keep yer taters up!" I only had enough time as I was rolling over to grab a string hanging down and take a tater. As soon as my hand went around the potato the beast hit me again with such force it knocked the breath out of me. I lay there not being able to breathe with who knows how much weight on top of me trying to rip my throat out. It's hard to breathe when the breath is knocked out of you and green saliva that tastes like rotten sulphurated eggs is filling your mouth.

The Boouke came for my neck with its mouth wide open. With the potato in hand, I prayed the quickest prayer I've ever prayed and I shoved my right arm into its mouth slicing my forearm as it rubbed against its razor-sharp teeth down into its gullet. I knew I would probably lose my arm but I was going to die anyway. If I did live by some miraculous feat of God, then I would sacrifice for my world as I knew it.

I pushed that potato as far as I could down its throat and said, "do your thing!" I let loose and in a split-second reaction, as I was pulling my arm out it chomped down and landed right on the joint of my right elbow!

I heard bones crush like dry leaves in the fall. I felt my flesh explode inside its mouth. I screamed so loud in excruciating pain! My arm was gone at the elbow! My right arm was GONE! Blood was squirting everywhere!

The Boouke jumped off me. With the potato lodged deeply in its throat, it began to cough and growl and spew green puke everywhere. Turning circles, it was disoriented. It began to puke up a black tar like substance all over the square. The men were ready, and I heard Robert Lee yell "FIRE!" They unleashed a barrage of pellets into the beast, the likes of which I hand never heard in my life. The beast was hit again but STILL very alive! Guns just seem no resistance against it! It lay down for a moment, then got up. Lay down then got up. As it rose a third time it was crouching on its hind quarters, coughing and spewing black tar everywhere.

Adam said, "Our guns are no use!"

Then, the Boouke just disappeared! Swoosh! VANISHED!

Chapter 17

The Battle of wills

It was eerily ghost silent. No one said a word. I was laying there crying out in so much pain absorbed in a conscious and unconscious struggle for life. It hurt to breathe. It hurt to lay there. I hardly knew what was happening.

Pa ran up to me and whipped his belt out of the loops and was immediately covered in my blood before he even got it wrapped around my arm like a tourniquet. That stopped the bleeding for the most part but I was in an out of consciousness that I barely remember it happening.

"Is it dead?" Adam asked.

Robert said, "I don't know! But until I see its mangey dead carcass on the ground I still ain't trusting it."

Everyone stood there for a good five minutes in silence. Hardly breathing, looking here and there waiting for it to re-appear any moment, but nothing.

Shelby said, "Maybe we killed it."

Joe Dilly responded, "I'm with Robert. I've got to see this thing dead for myself."

"IT'S NOT DEAD!"

"WHAT?" All the men looked at me in astonishment.

"It's not dead." I said.

"How do you know Will? What are you talking about?"

"I don't know." It took everything I had to breathe just to get enough breath to talk. I continued. "It's . . . on . . . its . . . way . . . back." I managed to say. I briefly passed out again. I woke up to Pa slapping my face gently saying, "Don't leave us Will!"

When I came to, I heard the question, "Will how do you know? When it is coming back?" Each man took turns asking these questions.

By this time, I was almost gone. Pa slapped my face a little more to keep me conscious. He was crying!

"Will, you have to stay with me. Will wake up! 'Dear Father, please provide a miracle for us and keep Will with us. Please save and heal him! God please take me instead! Amen!'"

After a few minutes I regained some consciousness and asked what had happened and where I was. Pa was stroking my head and praying softly.

"Pa . . . what's . . . going on?"

"Will, do you remember fighting the Boouke?"

My head fell to the side and looked away, "Yes."

"Will, you said you knew he wasn't dead. Can you tell me how you know that, son?"

I barely had the energy to breathe, much less to talk but I did my best. "When . . . I . . . had my hands . . . around . . . its neck . . ." I started to raise my hands to show what I did but forgot I didn't have a right arm and cried out in pain!

"It's ok," Pa said, "don't move, just talk if you can."

"When I . . . grabbed it, it looked at me . . . and I heard its thoughts. I saw its mind. It was dark . . .black . . . sickening and evil. But it's coming back." I continued to lay there in agony. The tenderness of the lacerations was warm with my life's blood oozing from them and my severed arm.

Robert said as calmly as he could, "Will, I know you're in pain but if you can, we need to know when this thing is coming back! Even if you have an inkling of an idea. Can you tell us?"

I didn't even have enough energy to turn my head. I stared up at the overhang on my porch, noticing places I need to fix I've never seen before. There was a spot I missed when I painted a few years ago. There's the swallow's nest, she comes back every year. It's covered in spider webs.

Pa said, "Will, Will!"

". . .What."

"Stay with us Will! Do you know when the Boouke is coming back?"

I eked out, ". . .soon." They were frustrated and I was dying. Swooning in and out of consciousness feeling weaker and weaker knowing I had probably minutes left.

"Pa? . . . Pa?"

"Yes Will…go on."

"Pa, I can't . . . see anything. Everything is going black. I'm . . .dying Pa. Tell Ma, Martha and the kids I love them. Pa, I love you." I felt my head slowly turn to the side and I breathed a long deep breath and relaxed.

Hardly able to talk Pa said, "I love you too son! I love you! But by God's will and my faith you ain't gonna die! YOU AIN'T GONNA DIE!" Pa was on his knees, holding me. He looked into the sky and yelled a prayer, "God! PLEASE SAVE WILL! He ain't gonna die!"

"I'm sorry Pa. Tell 'em I'll see 'em in heaven." I was in so much misery, I just wanted to die. In my dying moments I felt just enough breath and energy that I tried to yell out one last command with all I had, "COME BACK NOW YOU SORRY BEAST! COME FINISH ME OFF YOU COWARD!"

All of a sudden, black tar vomited out of its mouth on my face and all over Pa! I coughed and started puking all over the porch. Pa in a quick reaction jumped back and fell off the end of the porch.

THERE IT WAS! Right next to me, but it couldn't stop coughing and spewing black and green ooze, just like it was doing when it disappeared. Its grotesque undulating and my ability to see into its mind, told me it was in more pain than I was.

A sudden warmness came through me. I began to feel courage again! I felt strength coming back into my body! I was still in great pain, but strength! My eyes were clearing up! I could see. I slowly rolled over on my left side and leaned on my elbow and looked at the Boouke toward the front porch.

As soon as we locked eyes, I don't know how to explain this except that time stood still and we were both standing in some misty foggy room and neither of us were hurt. We were just standing and communicating to each other with our minds! Our mouths weren't even moving.

During this time, of which I really don't know how long it was, or where we were, it said to me, *"Will, listen to me. You know you are almost dead. Answer me honestly, do you want others to die?"*

I answered it, "No, I don't."

It said again, *"I have power over all the people. All I need is one more. If you will come with me, everyone will live and you will be their hero. No more death. You can save them by coming with me."*

Although I was not feeling any pain while this conversation was going on, I do remember how badly I was hurt. To be honest, its proposition really was very tempting but, I said, "I will never give up and I would NEVER go with you willingly. You will die Boouke!"

In violent anger still through its thoughts it said, *"You have no idea how long I've been coming here! I will eat you and everyone else unless you come with me!"*

I said back, "Whatever you are, you have no right here in our community. I will not let you leave. You will stay here until you die and go back to your home in hell!"

It smiled a most sinister grin and spoke to me almost peacefully and rationally. *"My home in hell?"* it began to laugh. *"You have no clue about me. I don't come from your so called "hell" I come from the stars and if I do happen to die, you have no idea what 'hell' is coming for you from the stars in the future!"*

I questioned it, "What are you?"

It laughed again. *"You don't even know where you are do you Will?"*

"What does that have to do with anything?" I said.

"Look around! You will see beings who are not like you Will. They are more advanced, stronger and have been here longer than any human dares to think. As for me, rarely do people see me in this, my true form. In my other form people have had many names for me down through the ages. They have tried to take pictures of me but I am uncatchable and unfindable! We live beyond your solar system. We are not subject to your laws of nature that you know of. There are many more dimensions and planes of existence of which you can't even conceive. That's why you are defeated Will. Come with me. You could not understand what I am if I were to tell you."

"Why do you only come to Three Rivers? Why not go somewhere else?"

"We do. We've been going all over the world for millennia. You are not the only ones. Come with us and your people will not have to go through this ever again!"

In my strongest thought I could muster up I said in my mind, "There is no hell coming for us because I will not let you leave! You will stay here until you die. Then we will live in peace. "

"LET ME GO!!!"

"NO! YOU WILL STAY UNTIL YOU DIE!"

This time it yelled out loud, "*NO!*" The men could tell something was going on but they could not hear us communicating mentally until the Boouke yelled an audible "NO!" Suddenly, we were out of the trance or vision or whatever it was. It was still spewing and coughing green and black liquid all over.

Pa ran over and for an old man I couldn't believe my eyes, in one leap he was on the porch again three steps high! Pa reached into his coat pocket and pulled out his Bible. Holding it up to the Boouke, it started to back up and growl amid its spewing and coughing.

"Keep it up Pete!" Yelled Robert Lee.

Shelby said excitedly, "Are you guys seeing what I'm seeing? Oh, my goodness!"

"What is that thing doing?" Said Joe Dilly.

"It's getting bigger! It's growing! Said Robert Lee.

"How we gonna fight and kill it if it gets bigger?" said, Adam.

Pa said, "Look, it's belly is getting huge!"

Shelby asked, "What's happening?"

"How do I know!?" responded Robert Lee. "I've never seen this before!"

The beast's belly continued to swell up. We could see it swell up larger and larger and larger. His whole body was growing! It was getting huge and we were scared all over again! It just kept growing until it was at least twelve to fifteen foot tall!

All the men began to yell at Pete. "Put your Bible up!" "It's making it grow, stop it Pete!" "Pete you're gonna' get us all kilt! Put it away!" It kept growing larger and larger!

"This thing is Massive boys!" Said Robert Lee in disbelief.

Shelby asked, "Do we run or stay?"

My Pa, his concentration on the Boouke and Bible still in hand holding it up as powerful as he could, said as loud as anyone, "WE STAY! My son is laying there dying without an arm, we're a stayin'!"

"We're agreed!" Yelled Robert. "But Pete you're making it grow bigger! Put 'yer Bible away!"

Pete said, "Boys, there are sometimes in life when you have to trust the Word of God even when it don't look like it's worth trusting!" He continued to hold the Bible up to the Boouke as it continued to grow like it was gaining strength and power from the Bible!

All the time this was going on, the beast was swelling and growing ever larger! Finally, it got so large that the Boouke, by now a good twenty-foot-tall, bigger than the imagination can even believe, gave one last sonic yell that almost burst all our ear drums! Its belly then burst forth with a supernatural like explosion.

Trees were bent over to the ground and many snapped right in two. Huge trees! All the men fell to the ground in fear and instant reaction. There was an echo throughout the mountains that sounded like a bag of dynamite all exploded at once!

Black tar, green puke and entrails went flying and flinging everywhere, end over end all over the square, and the whole surroundings for fifty feet around. Even all the men were covered with green entrails, slime, grey juices and strings of innards. Shards of bones flew like shrapnel into the trees and Lord knows whatever else came from that monster from the stars.

Although I was laying on the porch, the guts and gloppy green paste managed to cover me too. When it exploded I covered my head to protect myself. I heard something hard ricochet off the wall then it hit and penetrated my left arm that was covering my head. It hit with such a force and sharp pain so hard I almost passed out. I immediately grabbed for it with my other arm but it was gone! I could tell that whatever it was, each end of it was sticking out the top and bottom of my arm resting beside my bone.

I yelled in pain with what little strength I had left and cried and cried it hurt so bad! But there was too much going on at the time that I didn't think to look at it. After the explosion, I managed to raise my head and I looked at my arm and found that the object was none other than one of the Boouke's long teeth sticking all the way through my forearm where my head would have been had I not been covering it. Even in death, it tried one last time, through the explosion to kill me, but I was protected.

As the men lay there a minute, things went silent except for my moaning and the green mucus dripping off the limbs so much that it sounded like it was raining. Its bones were embedded in the trees like shards of metal. It's bowels and all the viscera were tangled and hanging down and swaying back and forth from the blast. I've never seen green barked trees, but we did that day. We just lay there not knowing if we were still in danger or not.

"Everyone ok?" Asked Robert Lee

They all agreed that they were ok and started coughing from the green saliva and the stench of the entrails all over us. Pa said, "I've skinned some stinky opossum in my day, but this takes the cake!"

All the men got up and ran over to me dirty and nasty as they could be. With a slight smile I said, "You guys stink!" They didn't know whether to laugh or cry.

"How are 'ya Will?" Robert asked. I said I was ok but they knew I wasn't and I knew I wasn't. I was hurt very bad, almost dead with one arm gone and almost bled out. My other arm has a Boouke tooth sticking out both sides. Not quite knowing how to grab me with an arm missing, they helped me up as blood was squirting everywhere and on everyone. I screamed in pain as Shelby grabbed my left arm, not knowing the tooth was sticking all the way through it.

"OH! I'm so sorry! What? You have a tooth sticking THROUGH your arm! I'm so sorry!"

I said, "It's ok, you didn't know." I continued in halting language, "Boys, if I survive all this and don't die from infection or blood loss it's gonna be a miracle."

Pa said, "It's already a miracle! You ain't gonna die son. God's got ya. He brung ya this far, He ain't a gonna' let you down now."

I just looked at my Pa and smiled.

Robert replied, "You know, I think your Pa just might be on to something with that God thing." We all smiled at him.

Joe Dilly chimed in, "Will, I do believe you are the strongest man I've ever met."

"No, I'm not strong Joe."

"Will, you're tough! You're a tough man. And 'tween you and me, I'd rather be tough than strong. You know that reminds me of the time when..."

"Not now Joe, we have to get this guy inside and keep him alive." Robert said with a smile.

They ran and got a sheet and put me in it and carried me into the house to my room. Even in my pain and nearly dead, I felt so bad for my wife Martha because my blood had already saturated the sheet and was squirting and dripping all over her house that she did such a great job of keeping clean for us.

"I'm sorry honey, for the mess I'm leaving, I'll clean it...."

"Don't you worry none about that William Jacob," my dear wife Martha scolded me gently. "That's nothing to be alarmed about. We'll get it."

Laying me down on my bed and pulling the sheet out from under me, Robert looked around and instinctively asked for Doc forgetting that he had been taken by the Boouke. We all felt bad. There was no doctor to work on me.

However, Adam said, "I have experience stitching up animals and some on people before. We've got to get will stitched up before infection sets in." I agreed as did the others. Randy ran to his father's office and brought his big medicine bag. Adam looked through it and the temporary doctor Adam went to work immediately. I was lacerated from head to toe. He worked on me for hours stopping every so often to let us both rest. The medicine we had and a good long snort of Robert's "White Lightnin," from up over the hill, every time we rested eased the edge off the pain a little.

When Adam was done, late into the night and morning, I had over 800 stitches from all the lacerations. The big deal was my arm. It was an absolute miracle from God but Adam got it to quit bleeding and sewed it up. Pouring that "White Lightnin" in all my lacerations and in my arm, well, that was almost a bit more than I could endure, but with my friends and family around me, giving me encouragement I was able to take it.

I was lovingly taken care of every single second of the day by my wife and others in the community who spelled her to give her some rest. Day after day after day, no one left my side. We have a great family at Three Rivers. The whole incident was unfortunate, but this just brought us closer.

The next day as dawn arose, we heard song birds singing and flitting back and forth in the trees as if nothing had happened. We saw the clouds, that lingered through the night, rising off Megan's hill and the moon made itself scarce along with the glorious stars in God's heaven as the warm sun came out to proclaim a new day.

During the night, through my window I had a glimpse up through the trees at small portion of the stars. I never told anyone, but in my mind, I said, "Boouke, if you were from the stars, like you said you were, I sure hope you don't have no brothers or sisters to come down here to revenge your death! But if they do. . .I'll have a 'tater waiting on them."

Yes, the Boouke was dead. Brought down by the lowly **potato.**

Chapter 18
Getting back to normal

Well, it has been a few months since I've written. I went back and finished the story starting where I left off, about the time I walked out on the porch. I have been laying here recovering the last several months going through the routine of replacing bandages, medicating the infections in my eyes and mouth from the saliva, and checking on and removing the stitches all over my body from the claws and teeth. I was treated as well as anyone could hope for. Every day, all the other families would take turns visiting me and bringing us food. The men would recount in glorious heroic detail, the story of what they saw. In a joking manner, each had a story of how "they" were the ones who brought down the Boouke.

I was sort of a hero with the young boys now. With his medical equipment, the new Doc Billy drilled a hole in the Boouke's tooth we had extruded from my arm and put a leather strip through it like a necklace. I keep that by my bedside. The young boys would come and visit me, more to see the tooth than for me I think. They are mezmorized by it as they hold it and examine it closely. A few of the men have too, but it was too real for them. They

192

don't want anything to do with it. Having fought the Boouke and won is quite an honor, but it came with a price to my body losing my arm, most of my strength and almost my life, but our community lost five heroic people that day.

I've laid here over the last few months sometimes wondering if it was real. Did that really happen? But the holes and scars in my body and my stump of an arm testify to the fact that the Boouke was real. It was real alright, October 29,1929 changed our lives forever in Three Rivers.

However, the Boouke is forever gone.

Robert Lee and Adam went to town a few weeks after the ordeal and because of something that happened in America, didn't have much trouble recruiting some more families to live in Three Rivers. When they returned they gathered the community together in the meeting house and described something that had happened to the United States that we had never heard of. They described it as a national de-pression.

"What's a de-pression?" Asked Martha.

Adam said, "Well, from the best we can figure, a de-pression is when nobody has any money at all and all the banks are out of money and there is no work for nobody. That's called a de-pression."

"What do people do to eat and work?" Asked Randy.

Adam continued, "Best we can figure, looks like they stand in line in front of stores and wait for soup and bread. As for work most of them don't. Others, they travel to other states and look for work mostly like California or Washington to pick crops for fifteen-cents a day."

"Is this de-pression going to hit us here?" Someone asked.

Robert said, "I don't see how, since we in Three Rivers don't operate on a bankin' system, and it started a few months ago and we didn't even know it so I doubt that it is going to affect us unless we go to town for something. Besides all our families have stashed away all our money many years ago when we got here, 'cause we don't use it here. So, if we do need to go to town, we'll have the money to buy what we need. Everything in town went real cheap because no one has any money to buy nothing! You want to hear something funny?"

Everyone agreed.

Robert said, "Adam, tell them about the conversation we had in Oscar's Dry Good's store."

"We walked in," Adam started telling the story, "And Oscar, who walks with a cane now recognized us from Three Rivers and got real nervous but was very polite. We did our shopping and went to the counter to settle up and here is the conversation that we had."

Robert said to Oscar, "Goodness, looks like these prices have dropped by half to three quarters since we've been in here last! You having a sell?"

Oscar looked at us with the strangest look and said, "You gentlemen haven't heard?"

"Heard what?" Asked Adam.

"October 29 last year of '29! The Stock Market Crashed. The whole United States is in a depression. Nobody has money, banks don't have no money, no jobs, nothing! My store here is about to go under because no one here has any jobs or money. Here, take a newspaper telling about it. You can read up on it yourself."

Robert responded, "Well I'll be. I don't understand the stock market but it sure must be important for it to affect the whole United States like that."

Oscar spoke up, "You folks in Three Rivers are lucky!"

"Why's that?"

"That day the market crashed? October 29, 1929 you were just living your life out there without a clue of the panic and devastation of what people were going through in the towns. Yes sir, it was so bad here on that day, you guys didn't have a clue as to how scary it was. I thought I'd never say this, but if there was one day I wish I were living in Three Rivers, it would have been That Tuesday, October 29, 1929. I would have been living my life without a worry in the world. Yep, that's the one day I'd choose to live there. You folks don't know how lucky you were on that Tuesday."

Adam, addressing us in our assembly now, telling the story said, "Me and Robert looked at each other and Robert said, "Yes, Mr. Oscar, I do believe you are right in one aspect. We sure were lucky and I might even say blessed on that day in Three Rivers, but maybe for different reasons than you might suspect. But trust me sir, you were in the right place on that Tuesday just where you were supposed to be. I'm sorry to hear about this depression but I believe all of us if we pull together, we can make it. In fact, Mr. Oscar, here is twenty extra dollars to help keep the store open. We'll do our part to help with this depression."

Oscar stood there looking at us with tears starting to come down his cheeks. "I can't believe you gentlemen, just did that! Do you know how much twenty dollars is worth right now? This is like gold! Thank you! Thank you very much!"

"You're welcome," said Robert. As we exited Robert turned around and said, "Mr. Oscar?"

"Yes sir?"

"Keep yer' tater's up!"

"What?" Oscar said confused.

"It's something we say in Three Rivers. It means 'stay safe."

"Oh!" Said Oscar. "Well then, you keep your potatoes' up too!"

We laughed and left and started on our way home. Adam continued talking to our assembly, "I believe it's good for us to know what is going on in the world, but since this de-pression ain't affecting us, there's no need for us to worry about it. We just wanted to let you know how blessed we are to live here with such good people as ourselves. "AAAAmen." Everyone said.

Martha spoke up in the assembly, "Excuse me, I can't help but wonder, since the Boouke and this de-pression happened on the same day, do you think the Boouke caused that too?"

"It's hard to say, Martha." Adam said. Everyone in the world knows about the de-pression. Nobody knows about the Boouke except us and, well, let's just keep it that way." Martha smiled.

Even though three of our men (besides Elsa and Dane Jr.) died at the violence of the Boouke, Robert and Adam recruited four. Three weeks after everything was over, my Pa died in his sleep with his Bible on his chest as he read from it before he closed his eyes for the last time. His reading glasses were still on. I suspected he knew he was going, because on a piece of paper sticking out of his Bible he had written me a note.

I could barely read it through the tears filling my eyes and streaming down my face. Sobbing deeply from love I began to read the letter.

Dear Will, you were God's David against Goliath. One-time God used a little stone, this time God used a little potato. It doesn't matter what it is, what matters is that we serve God and do our best with what He gives us. I'm so sorry you are torn up the way you are, but I couldn't be prouder of you if you were my own blood son. Take care of Ma and give little James and Katie a kiss for me every morning. Tell them their Papaw misses them and will see them later in heaven. Remind them and the others that the Word of God will help you through evil times. That's what it says in the Good Book and that's good enough for me. I will see you later too. Keep your taters up.

Love eternally, your Pa.

I laid my head on the top of the Bible laying on his chest and just cried. I was so thankful for all that he was to me and the examples he set through my life. The top of the Bible was a lake of tears when I got up. I was wrong when I said the Poe book or Washington's chair was the greatest gift I ever received. As I get older, I am seeing things from a little different perspective. The greatest gift was having Pete and Millie for my Pa and Ma. But then there is my wife Martha, my kids and all the relationships I have developed over the years. Especially the one Pa lived out every day, and I now have for myself, a relationship with God. Still not sure the other men "get it" but I did.

As for Ma, she seems so lost. Being married over sixty-three years and loosing one half of you is devastating and lonely. She asks me and Martha about things that she would have normally rolled up her sleeves and done prior to Pa's death. She is so unsure of herself now. She cries a lot and I'm so glad we are here to just be family when we each needed it. Lord knows they became my "family" when I needed it.

I feel so bad for her loss but her determination to go on and her trust in God is a great lesson to me and my family as well as the families in Three Rivers. She reads the Bible to the kids every night and she almost always says, "And Pa used to say…" then she would expound on some scripture as Pa saw it. Before she finishes, she took on something new and now says, "That's what it says in the Good Book and that's good enough for me. Amen."

She now makes all my family big "cat-head" biscuits every morning! We call them that because they are as big as cat heads! Every morning before the kids get up, Ma delivers them with butter and sorghum molasses in the quart jar she canned last fall. Sorghum makin' is a community event. In September or October, whenever it is ready, I love cutting the sugar cane then putting it between the rollers in the crushing machine to extract the green juice. As I'm cutting, I'll often take a small stalk and chew it between my teeth to extract the sweet sugary syrup as I work. That is a small tantalizing taste of what is to come.

We then take that juice to Ma and the other ladies in the community and they cook it the next day, thickening it into a light amber syrup that darkens into a thick dark brown molasses, that is then canned or sealed in a quart jar. Ten gallons of raw sorghum juice yields about one gallon of syrup. However, in my opinion, all the work is worth it! There is nothing and I do mean nothing better than a cat-head biscuit with butter and molasses. I do hope the Good Lord serves that in heaven for us.

The four new families have visited me already and I think we're going to get along very well. The men made good choices on the new arrivals. When the new families saw me in my condition, I'm sure they wondered what they got into and probably had second thoughts. We assured them the Boouke was gone forever and from now on we have nothing to worry about except taking care of our own community and living in peace.

I look terrible with scars and cuts from my face to my feet. Part of my skin on my skull was ripped off by the Boouke so I have a big patch of white skull bone showing. We're keeping that bandaged hoping skin grows back over it. I am watching out for infection. A couple of days after sewing me up, the new Doc, Billy, they recruited found a couple of my fingers broken and disjointed and he "popped" them back into place. That hurt like the dickins but they look and feel better now. I still walk with a limp, perhaps I always will but I take that as an honor. I saved my family and the community, not by my choice but by courageous actions that any man in our community would have displayed if they were in my situation. It just happens to be me it attacked at that time.

I am also grateful to my little son James, who left his "monster sword" just in the right place. It allowed me to help kill the monster. God answered my prayer for a sword. I have it hanging up above the fireplace and I look at it every day. Perhaps there will come a time when I will not think about it, but not today. We found James another "monster stick."

Joe Dilly's daughter Judith never was right after wondering off into the woods and brought back. She improved her communication skills a little for a shallow conversation but she doesn't talk much. No one can get her to say anything more than what she already said about why she walked out there, who led her, or what she meant by seeing Elsa "floating" above her house. We think, that whatever she saw, was so horrific that it scared the living rational wits right out of her head. A person can only take so much before it starts to affect them. However, Joe Dilly and his wife are so glad to have her back. They do a real good job of taking care of her and being patient.

We've taken down all the potatoes except one on every house, so we will always remember our effort, teamwork and those who perished. Joe Dilly carved a wooden plaque and hung it on the tree in the middle of the square with the names of Doc Carl, Elsa, Joshua, Dane and D.J. (Dane Jr.). We call it "Five- Hero's Square." In humor and honor of me the sign has a hand holding up "five" fingers for my right arm the Boouke chomped off.

Martha and I had a good long talk several weeks ago about something that is very dear to me. We discussed this important matter with our children James and Madison. We felt like we wanted to carry on the legacy of my Pa and Ma, Pete and Millie. So, with the discussion of the council and agreement of two young boys, we adopted Matt and Randy as our children just like I was adopted when I was little. It's hard. They are older than I was and there is some adjustment to be made on both sides but they seem to be happy living with what the boys call, "The Boouke Killer." We make a good family of six. By the way, Matt and Randy have fallen in love with Ma's biscuits and molasses. They are boys after my own heart. I'm sure going to miss her sweet smile and love when she's gone.

As I re-read the whole story, I remember sitting down early that morning and beginning to write when the ordeal started. I would not have given you a plug nickel to bet I'd be alive at the end of that day, much less to be the one to kill the Boouke. But, as Pa said, "God has a way of working all things out for good." I sure hope I'm half the man that my Pa was.

Even though I'm all torn up I feel so blessed by God that He brought me through and enabled me to have the wits, courage and power to defeat the Boouke. Every time someone thinks about it now, they shake their head in wonder and ask, "Will, how'd 'ya do it?"

I always say, "With God's strength." Beowulf said, *"Often, for undaunted courage, fate spares the man it has not already marked."*

Now that it's over, I lay in bed at night holding that tooth that almost went through my skull and I stare up at the stars and wonder where its family is, when they are coming back and if it's really over. But I keep those thoughts to myself.

"Keep your taters up."

Signed, William.

P.S.: Read some Poe.

Epilogue: Author's note: Well, there you have it. You have read it as it was written back in 1929. Do we have the answer to the Dyatlov tragedy? Are the answers to 'Big Foot' mystery close to being solved? Is this why the 'Big Foot' cannot be found and documented because he is a morph of the Boouke and then disappears? With all the "alien" information and number of sightings going on now, are we ominously close to a visit from the Boouke's species as warned?

I had one last question to this gentleman who gave me the journal, "Do you still have the 'tooth' that your descendant kept, that almost killed him?" I waited with my breath held as he looked down and reached into his pocket. My heart began to pound so hard and I could tell my breathing was getting louder.

"Well, Dan, here's what I have." He held his hand out upside down. I held my hand under his and he dropped it onto my palm into my hand. I was literally shaking. I brought it back and looked at it with wide eyes and amazement.

"This is it huh?" I said quietly.

"Well, Dan, I know you are going to be disappointed, but this is a deer antler that's been carved into a replica of that tooth."

My heart sank. "So, this is not the original tooth." I just had to ask one more time to confirm this was not the real tooth.

"No, I'm sorry." He said

"Ok, then," I have to ask, "Do you know where the original tooth went?"

"I was told," he continued, "That the original tooth was buried with our descendant as was his families' request. I know what you are thinking, but we do not know where he is buried. There's no way to find the grave to dig it up and try to find the tooth."

"Well, Mr. --------, I have to ask one more question and I hope you do not take this as personally offensive, but are you just hiding the fact that you don't want anyone to see or have the real tooth or do you really not know where it is or where he is buried?"

"I can assure you Dan, I'm not offended and we really do not know where the tooth or the burial plot is. I promise." He said with a confident smile. I trusted him.

As I stated in my introduction the two years following my meeting with the descendant of William Jacob MacAoidh consumed my life with reading and research. So enamored I was with the concept of the

Boouke changing into a "Big Foot" like creature, I began researching the "Big Foot" throughout history to see if there was a connection between the wording or concept of a large 'Ape' type man and 'aliens' or 'star people.'

The stories of the 'Sasquatch' and reported 'man like or ape like' creatures, have been part of the Northwestern American history for generations. The native American Indians have stories of the Wendigo, meaning 'the evil spirit that devours mankind.' The North West Coast Peoples and First Nation Peoples have shared with me that they do not remember a time when the Wendigo story was not told.

Were these stories real? How certain were these peoples that the 'creature' was real? A Wendigo reportedly went to Rosesu in Northern Minnesota from the late 1800's to the 1920's. Each time it was reported that it went to town, a death or disappearance was reported and then it was seen no more. Even in the last century, Native Americans actively believed in and searched for the Wendigo.

In the Pacific Northwest the Yakama Indians had a tradition of the 'Qah-lin-me'-a people devourer. Another name was 'Omah' used by the Hupa Indians that means wilderness demon. The Nisqually in western Washington

called it 'Tsiatko" which was a giant, hairy beast.
Certainly, this concept of a 'Big Foot' like creature crosses cultures, times, people's and locations. Chinese reports a huge giant hairy creature as early as 200 b.c..

One area of interest and high reports of seeing a large hairy type man was and is in British Columbia, Canada. I will spare all the details, except for two stories, one of the Chapman's in 1941 and the other of an Anasazi story of the American Southwest around 800 a.d..

You can look up these happenings if you are interested but I will list several incidents going back to 1783:

1783- James K. Smith found footprints in the snow measuring fourteen inches long by eight inches wide.

1864- Alexander Caulfield of the Hudson's Bay Trading Co had his party attacked by hairy humanoids by having rocks thrown at them from the cliffs above.

1871- Chehalis Indian woman was abducted by a Sasquatch from the Harrison Mills Community and was able to escape and tell her story.

1900- Restoration Bay, several witnesses saw a Sasquatch on the river beach which retreats into the forest when it knew it was being watched.

1909- Maclean's Magazine April 1, 1920 reports the story of a Sasquatch, in 1909 chased a group of people across the Chehalis River, followed one home and shoved him against the wall of his house.

1930- Greg Dorcy and a group of loggers at Fort St. John hear awful screaming during the night. With lights they spot a Sasquatch lurking around their camp. They shot at it and thought they saw it limp off into the forest. It was never found.

1940- Lookout Bay a man by the name of T.Y. saw a seven to eight-foot hairy creature walking along the beach into a grove of trees.

The first happening I will elaborate on happened in 1946- According to Ivan T. Sanderson, *True Magazine*, March 1960, I quote, "The Chapman family consisted of George and Jeannie Chapman and children numbering, at my visit, four. Mr. Chapman worked on the railroad and was living at that time in a small place called Ruby Creek, 30 miles up the Fraser River from Agassiv, British Columbia, in Canada's great western province.

It was about 3 in the afternoon of a sunny, cloudless day when Jeannie Chapman's eldest son, then aged 9, came running to the house saying that there was a cow coming down out of the woods at the foot of the nearby mountain.

The other kids, a boy aged 7 and a little girl of 5, were still playing in a field behind the house bordering on the rail track.

Mrs. Chapman went out to look, since the boy seemed oddly disturbed, and they saw what at first, she thought was a very big bear moving about among the bushes bordering the field beyond the railway tracks. She called the two children who came running immediately. Then the creature moved onto the tracks and she saw to her horror that it was a gigantic man covered with hair, not fur. The hair seemed to be about four inches long all over, and of a pale yellow-brown color. To pin down this color Mrs. Chapman pointed out to me a sheet of lightly varnished plywood in the room where we were sitting. This was of a brown-ochre color.

This creature advanced directly toward the house and Mrs. Chapman had, as she put it, "much too much time to look at it" because she stood her ground outside while the eldest boy — on her instructions — got a blanket from the house and rounded up the other children. The kids were in a near panic, she told us, and it took two or three minutes to get the blanket, during which time the creature had reached the near corner of the field only about 100 feet away from her. Mrs. Chapman then spread the blanket and, holding it aloft so that the kids could not see the creature or it them, she backed off at the double to the old field and down on to the river beach out of sight, and then ran with the kids downstream to the village.

Mrs. Chapman told me that the creature was about 7½ feet tall. She could estimate its height by the various fence and line posts standing about the field. It had a rather small head and a very short, thick neck; in fact, really no neck at all, a point that was emphasized by William Roe and by all others who claim to have seen one of these creatures. Its body was entirely human in shape except that it was immensely thick through its chest and its arms were exceptionally long. She did not see the feet which were in the grass. Its shoulders were very wide and it had no breasts, from which Mrs. Chapman assumed it was a male, though she also did not see any male genitalia due to the long hair covering its groin. She was most definite on one point: the naked parts of its face and its hands were much darker than its hair and appeared to be almost black.

George Chapman returned home from his work on the railroad that day shortly before 6 in the evening and by a route that by-passed the village so that he saw no one to tell him what had happened. When he reached his house he immediately saw the woodshed door battered in, and spotted enormous humanoid footprints all over the place. Greatly alarmed — for he, like all of his people, had heard since childhood about the "big wild men of the mountains," though he did not hear the word Sasquatch till after this incident — he called for his family and then dashed through the house. Then he spotted the foot-tracks of his wife and kids going off toward the river. He followed these until he picked them up on the sand beside the river and saw them going off downstream without any giant ones following.

Somewhat relieved, he was retracing his steps when he stumbled across the giant's foot-tracks on the river bank farther upstream. These had come down out of the potato patch, which lay between the house and the river, had milled about by the river, and then gone back through the old field toward the foot of the mountains where they disappeared in the heavy growth.

Returning to the house, relieved to know that the tracks of all four of his family had gone off downstream to the village, George Chapman went to examine the woodshed. In our interview, after 18 years, he still expressed voluble astonishment that any living thing, even a 7-foot-6- inch man with a barrel-chest could lift a 55-gallon tub of fish and break it open without using a tool. He confirmed the creature's height after finding a number of long brown hairs stuck in the slab wood lintel of the doorway, above the level of his head.

George Chapman then went off to the village to look for his family and found them in a state of calm collapse. He gathered them up and invited his father-in-law and two others to return with him, for protection of his family when he was away at work.

The foot-tracks returned every night for a week and on two occasions the dogs that the Chapmans had taken with them set up the most awful racket at exactly 2 o'clock in the morning. The Sasquatch did not, however, molest them or, apparently, touch either the house or the woodshed. But the whole business was too unnerving, and the family finally moved out. They never went back.

After a long chat about this and other matters, Mrs. Chapman suddenly told us something very significant just as we were leaving. She said: "It made an awful funny noise." I asked her if she could imitate this noise for me but it was her husband who did so, saying that he had heard it at night twice during the week after the first incident. He then proceeded to utter exactly the same strange, gurgling whistle that the men in California, who said they had heard a Bigfoot call, had given us. This is a sound I cannot reproduce in print, but I can assure you that it is unlike anything I have ever heard given by man or beast anywhere in the world."

The Chapman's house at Ruby Creek

Are these interactions really, people seeing the Boouke having come to earth in its 'morphed' form? The similarities are overwhelming in the fact that it has been documented for 100's of years, it is almost documented with exactly the same description, the footprints are almost always within the same size, it cannot be caught, killed, or captured. There has been no ultimate unrefuted proof of a physical body even when people say they have killed it. Even back in 1929 when it exploded. We only have the testimony of the journal. This monster's similarities continue by the fact that it either ravages and kills or captures by abduction. Then most of the time, it is not seen for a long time.

In interviewing many tribal leaders from many tribes over the U.S., I came across the second happening I want to elaborate on. Perhaps it is the greatest and most compelling story that comes from the Anasazi Community, in the Four-Corners area of the American Southwest around 800 A.D. I was told the following story, by a tribal chief, in secret, directly passed down from generation to generation orally until it was written down in the late 1800's. When I met with him, I was certain not to tell him about the journal or the creature so I would get no cross contamination of stories or suggest items he might interject for my story. I only asked if he knew anything about star people and Sasquatch and if they were linked somehow.

Before the tribal Chief began to tell his story, he lit a bundle of sage and chanted a protection blessing on the house, himself and especially me, he said. He mixed the sage smoke around with a big feather and swept it over on me because he could feel I was stirring up a spirit of the one he was going to speak about. As we sat one on one, he began to tell the story and as I saw the look of fear on his face as he told it, startled me to my inner core. I could not believe the similarities between his story and the one you just read. I was literally shaking as I was writing.

You be the judge. With great voice inflections and hand gestures, he began the story. . .

"Wind-Tree, bowing in submission and honor, makes his way into the Shaman's cave and kneels in silence.

"Speak, Wind-Tree. You may get up."

"Holy Shaman, may I ask how you see and know it is me from behind the hanging blanket? It is thick!"

"I am Shaman. I need no eyes to see. Get up and speak."

"Holy Shaman, I have news from the community. The foul smell is still in the air but Deer Knifekiller has found a way he thinks will destroy Wee-Tee-Go Booukie. For some reason, Wee-Tee-Go Booukie fears the potato."

"The potato? How does he know this?"

"Holy Shaman, we were successful in shooting arrows into Wee-Tee-Go Booukie but it was doing no good. We were running out of arrows and as a last effort, we began reaching into the basket throwing potatoes at Wee-Tee-Go Booukie knowing it would be of no use. But as we

did, it began to yell and run away. When we would stop, it would return with a vengeance. Deer Knifekiller says we can dip our arrows in potato juice and shoot Wee-Tee-Go Booukie so the juice acts like a poison.

Chief Bear-Walk says we can do nothing without Holy Shaman's permission. This is why I am here. Would you like us to kill Wee-Tee-Go Booukie Holy Shaman?"

"Wind-Tree tell them 'NO!' You must not kill Wee-Tee-Go Booukie"

"WHAT?! BUT ME MUST!"

"Do you defy my word Wind-Tree?!"

Falling and lying flat on the ground Wind-Tree said in repentance, "I'm sorry Holy Shaman, please forgive me. I was disrespectful."

"Get up, you must tell Chief Bear-Walk and Deer Knifekiller my vision. Last night in my communications with the gods, I saw in my vision Wee-Tee-Go Booukie. As it came down from the star people it fought us, and for what reason, even I do not know. It was killed by Deer Knifekiller before it could ascend back into the stars. All the people rejoiced because it was gone and there was no more fear of Wee-Tee-Go Booukie forever. It was a period of peace.

"That's good Holy Shaman! Let us kill it!"

"NO! The vision revealed that when Wee-Tee-Go Booukie is dead, there is one to come after it that is many times more evil than Wee-Tee-Go Booukie itself. Let it live. Tell them to keep fighting it until its time is over then it will ascend back to its own star people.

"The vision told me that many moon cycles from now, Wee-Tee-Go Booukie will descend from the stars again but it will be killed and sometime later the Powerful One from the star people will come and try to destroy all things as revenge. May the gods have a good heart toward those who kill Wee-Tee-Go Booukie, they will need it."

"Yes, Holy Shaman. I will relay this to Chief Bear-Walk and Deer Knifekiller."

"Go, Wind-Tree. Tell them, whatever they do, do NOT kill Wee-Tee-Go Booukie! That is the worst thing that could happen."

"Yes, Holy Shaman."

"Go in peace Wind-Tree."

THE END?